Samuel French Acting Edition

I0584689

Thespian Playworks 2012

507
by Natasha Sowka

Circuits
by Rachel Lepore

South of Someplace
by I.B. Hopkins

Shelf Life
by Beth Seeley

SAMUELFRENCH.COM   SAMUELFRENCH.CO.UK

FOR PRODUCTION ENQUIRIES

UNITED STATES AND CANADA
Info@SamuelFrench.com
1-866-598-8449

UNITED KINGDOM AND EUROPE
Plays@SamuelFrench.co.uk
020-7255-4302

Each title is subject to availability from Samuel French, depending upon country of performance. Please be aware that *THESPIAN PLAYWORKS 2012* may not be licensed by Samuel French in your territory. Professional and amateur producers should contact the nearest Samuel French office or licensing partner to verify availability.

MUSIC USE NOTE

Licensees are solely responsible for obtaining formal written permission from copyright owners to use copyrighted music in the performance of this play and are strongly cautioned to do so. If no such permission is obtained by the licensee, then the licensee must use only original music that the licensee owns and controls. Licensees are solely responsible and liable for all music clearances and shall indemnify the copyright owners of the play(s) and their licensing agent, Samuel French, against any costs, expenses, losses and liabilities arising from the use of music by licensees. Please contact the appropriate music licensing authority in your territory for the rights to any incidental music.

IMPORTANT BILLING AND CREDIT REQUIREMENTS

If you have obtained performance rights to this title, please refer to your licensing agreement for important billing and credit requirements.

FOREWORD

"Playwriting," according to nineteen-year-old rising talent Rachel Lepore, "is mixing fantastic circumstances with realistic characters, and striving to impart your message to the audience."

Sounds simple enough, right? But every year around this time, as we sift through dozens of student submissions from across the country in hopes of finding four stageworthy scripts for Thespian Playworks, my colleagues and I are reminded just how tough it is for a teen-ager – for anyone – to achieve this triple feat that Rachel defines so succinctly: An imaginative story. Characters we can believe in. A play with something to say. Even in the professional world, most playwriting attempts fail on at least one count; we Playworks judges, on our crankiest days, sometimes wonder whether these kids are competing to see who can bomb most spectacularly on all three, though we always receive some wonderful entries as well. (I admit to a particular fondness for the disasters – probably because I wrote more than a few of them myself, back when I was in school.)

Last year, four especially bright high school seniors pulled off, in four very different ways, the playwright's simple-if-it-weren't-so-impossible task. In *Circuits,* Rachel Lepore drew a typical sibling rivalry – irresponsible jock versus uptight brain – redeemed by love and acceptance after the older brother's accidental death. I.B. Hopkins, making his second Playworks appearance with *South of Someplace,* envisioned a generational clash in the garden of a crumbling Southern mansion. In Beth Seeley's *Shelf Life,* the delicate residents of a doll museum discovered the joys – and the costs – of freedom. And within the close confines of a generic New York hotel room known only as *507,* Natasha Sowka threw together three girls, a guy, and a strategically placed bathroom door.

These compelling situations, characters, and themes all deserved a life beyond the page. So last June we brought Rachel, Isaac, Beth, and Natasha, and a team of professional directors and dramaturg/mentors, to the Thespian Festival on the University of Nebraska campus. We recruited student actors and stage managers and put everyone through four frenzied days of workshop rehearsals and rewrites, culminating in an afternoon of performances for an audience that definitely got the message. I'll never forget the collective "Oh!" when an Old South patriarch revealed his true identity, the gasps when one doll's off-shelf adventures came crashing to an end, or the laughter when the unlikely lovers of *507* found themselves on opposite sides of yet another hotel-room door. And when our imaginary curtain fell on *Circuits,* with Emily, finally alone in her room, hugging her brother's football to her chest, I had to get up and hand out tissues: people were *weeping.* And cheering. "Seeing that final scene during our staged reading," Rachel told me in a recent email, "was easily one of the highest points of my life."

Launched in 1994 by the Educational Theatre Association and run by the staff of *Dramatics* magazine, Playworks began as a tribute to long-time International Thespian Society executive Doug Finney. Samuel French, Inc. has been a major sponsor of the program since 2009, and this anthology, the third of its kind, strikes me as another standing ovation, in paper form. It says to these talented young playwrights, "You did it. We liked it. We hope you'll do it again."

No worries there: every time I check in with a former Playworks finalist, he or she seems to be writing a new play. "It's like now that I've started," Natasha confessed in our last email exchange, "I just can't stop." Rachel, Isaac, and Beth said much the same.

A bit more about them: A graduate of the Las Vegas Academy, Rachel Lepore is now developing her craft at Playwright's Horizons Theatre School at New York University. I.B. Hopkins graduated from Gainesville High School and is now at the University of Georgia, majoring in English and theatre. A graduate of Anderson High School in Cincinnati, Beth Seeley is at Kenyon College, studying drama, psychology, and anthropology. And Natasha Sowka, a graduate of Cypress Lake High School in Cape Coral, Florida, is earning credit at Edison State College before moving on to a B.A. program in film and writing.

Natasha calls playwriting "one of the scariest and most rewarding art forms." For these four plays and their creators, at least, the scary part is over (for now). We're so proud of these student writers, and grateful to our friends at Samuel French, Inc., for sweetening their reward.

– *Julie York Coppens*
Senior Associate Editor,
Dramatics magazine
March 2013

CONTENTS

507

by Natasha Sowka

507 was presented in a staged reading as part of the Thespian Playworks program at the 2012 Thespian Festival. Joe Norton directed and Dominic Orlando was the dramaturg.

ELLIOT .... Jon Barnes
IRENE .... Haley Gardner
AVERY ....Nick Rice
JEN .... Kaitlyn Barret

ABOUT THE PLAYWRIGHT

Natasha Sowka is a playwright and photographer currently based out of Florida. At the age of twelve she saw a production of *Barefoot in the Park* and fell in love with the theatre. She has been reading, writing, and performing plays ever since. She is a graduate of Cypress Lake High School Center for the Arts where she studied dramatic arts. She plans to pursue the art of writing and directing in college and beyond. In 2012 she was selected, out of a pool of students, as one of the four playworks finalists for her one-act *507*. She is the author of four one-act plays however, *507* is her first published work.

CHARACTERS

ELLIOT - Male, mid-twenties. An average young man, good humor, mildly sarcastic.

IRENE - Female, mid-twenties. Avery's friend, quick-witted, loyal.

AVERY - Female, mid-twenties. Eccentric, spontaneous, wildly smart.

JEN - Female, mid-twenties. Elliot's girlfriend, quick-tempered, hard working.

(A small hotel room in New York City. The room consists of one large bedroom and a bathroom to the left of the main room. ELLIOT is on stage, standing near the edge of the bed. The phone rings and he sprints to grab it.)

ELLIOT. Hi? Hello! Hey! Jen? Jen, can you hear me? Yeah. No it's pretty loud on your end. What? I can't – okay.

(He waits a moment.)

Yeah that's better. I didn't mean to interrupt. Well see, that's the thing, I'm not. No. I'm in New York. Jen stop yelling. Jen – What? Of course not! Yes, I know. Well I figured you could get out of it. I didn't think it was – you know what, never mind, it's not that big of a deal anyway. Well, can you blame me? I'm only here for a week. I thought you'd want to see me. No. No I'm –

(Shouting is heard from offstage. ELLIOT pauses a minute to listen before continuing on the phone.)

Look, this isn't a conversation I want to have over the phone. Can you just come to the hotel so I can see you? The one near that diner you showed me last time I came. Yeah. Of course I remember. I know. I miss you too. Just come soon.

(ELLIOT takes a room key out of his pocket and looks at it. He puts the key back in his pocket.)

Room 507.

(The shouting gets louder, until it is just outside the door.)

So how's that new project going?

(The door starts rattling as if someone is trying to open it from the outside.)

Hey, could you hold on a second? No, everything's fine. Just some people in the hall are –

(ELLIOT opens the door and AVERY bursts into the room. She heads directly into the bathroom and slams the door shut. IRENE follows close behind her and tries to open the door, only to find that it is locked.)

ELLIOT. *(simultaneously with IRENE, overlapping)* You know what, I'll you call back. No I'll call you right back. Can you please – No I'm not trying to hang – Jen seriously just let me –

IRENE. *(at the bathroom door, simultaneous, overlapping)* Come on open the door, you can't lock yourself in there forever. Are you even listening to me? You're acting like a child –

(ELLIOT hangs up the phone abruptly.)

ELLIOT. *(overlapping)* Miss, you're in my room. Are you listening to me? Could you please do this somewhere else?

IRENE. You can't lock yourself in every room you come across. Can we please just go home and forget this all happened? Okay, I get it. You're angry, I –

ELLIOT. *(louder, over IRENE)* Excuse me, can I help you?

IRENE. I'm kind of in the middle of something right now.

ELLIOT. Yeah, my hotel room.

IRENE. Can you just give me a minute? Avery, come on we have to go. Please just come out.

AVERY. *(from behind the bathroom door)* You called me crazy.

IRENE. Crazy was back in the hallway, this is just ridiculous.

AVERY. The crazy lady doesn't feel like discussing it anymore.

IRENE. Are you really going to act like a five-year old?

(She pauses. There is no answer.)

Fine then, have it your way.

(IRENE turns to ELLIOT.)

Do you have a hair pin?

ELLIOT. Excuse me?

IRENE. Thin, small, goes in your hair.

ELLIOT. Do I look like I have a hair pin?

IRENE. Okay fine. How about a knife? A credit card?

(*He looks at her skeptically.*)

To open the door with – Do you want her out or not?

(**ELLIOT** *looks in his pockets. After a second he takes out the room key and hands it to* **IRENE.** **IRENE** *grabs it and starts messing around with the door, trying to open it.*)

AVERY. Did you know you can pick a lock with a soda can? It's crazy what you can find on the internet these days. Ever seen a cat ride a Roomba?

IRENE. You're not helping.

AVERY. You have to curve it when you jam the card in.

(*pause*)

Maybe it only works from this side. Here, let me try.

(**IRENE** *slides the card under the door.* **AVERY** *grabs it but makes no move to open the door. After a second* **IRENE** *realizes her mistake.*)

IRENE. When I get in there –

ELLIOT. Can you and your friend sort this out somewhere else?

AVERY. We're not friends.

IRENE. You're overreacting!

AVERY. (*mockingly*) You're overreacting!

IRENE. Avery, open the door!

AVERY. Sorry. I don't think I'm sane enough to work a door handle.

IRENE. That's it.

(**IRENE** *makes her way towards the hotel room door.*)

ELLIOT. Where are you going?

IRENE. You can keep King George. I've reached my limit.

ELLIOT. Wait…mental patient? You can't just leave.

IRENE. Isn't that what you just asked me to do?

ELLIOT. There's a person locked in my bathroom.

IRENE. That's not my problem anymore. Smoke her out or something.

ELLIOT. You can't be serious.

(IRENE *exits.* ELLIOT *makes his way back over to the bathroom door and speaks through it.*)

Miss, are you okay in there?

AVERY. You have a nice bathroom. It's very accommodating.

ELLIOT. Thanks, I guess.

AVERY. You know some people don't take the time to really look at a bathroom, always in a rush, you know? I don't know much about proper bathroom structure but it's nice, good tile. I'm not so keen on the wallpaper, though. It throws off the whole design scheme. It's very Dorothy Draper. I'd add one of those funky little cabinets and maybe a rug. It'd have to be some shade of blue to balance out the wallpaper though. What do you think?

ELLIOT. You're analyzing a bathroom?

AVERY. You can learn a lot about a person from their bathroom. Mine has a walk-in shower.

ELLIOT. It's not my bathroom. We're in a hotel.

AVERY. That makes more sense. It's very feminine, doesn't fit you at all.

ELLIOT. Well, your friend is –

AVERY. Unless you're a girl, in which case I'm really sorry. You don't sound like a girl. Oh god, that came out wrong. I'm sorry...again. Are you a girl?

ELLIOT. Not the last time I checked.

AVERY. That's good. You can never be too sure. Who are you anyway?

ELLIOT. Elliot. You're kind of in my bathroom.

AVERY. I thought you said it wasn't yours.

ELLIOT. What?

AVERY. The bathroom – you said it wasn't yours.

ELLIOT. I paid for the room, including the bathroom.

AVERY. So it is yours.

ELLIOT. I guess you could say that.

AVERY. You don't make a lot of sense. I'm sorry. That was rude. *(pause)* I know you probably think I'm crazy. I come off as a bit crazy at first but I have a very endearing personality. Everyone always tells me that. I'm Avery by the way.

ELLIOT. Your friend is gone. Do you think maybe you could come out?

AVERY. I've had a long night.

ELLIOT. I doubt an evening in my bathroom can help you with that.

AVERY. You doubt the power of a properly furnished bathroom. I know it's a lot to ask but would you mind if I just stayed in here for a little bit? I just like it in here. I don't even mind the wallpaper so much anymore. I won't steal anything. Your soap is safe with me.

ELLIOT. That's comforting, really.

(There is a silence as **ELLIOT** *thinks.)*

AVERY. I won't be long. I promise. You won't even notice I'm here.

ELLIOT. I'd notice if I had to use the bathroom.

AVERY. You could always use the one downstairs. Or in my room, wherever that is.

ELLIOT. So you do have a room?

AVERY. Of course I do. I don't spend my time gallivanting around random hotels, hopping from room to room. I'm not crazy. Well, I'm not that crazy.

ELLIOT. Of course you're not crazy. You have an endearing personality.

AVERY. I think I'm room 607.

ELLIOT. This is 507. You're one floor off.

AVERY. I must have missed that last flight. People always tell me that, you know? About my personality, that it's endearing.

ELLIOT. I do know, you told me. That's why I said it.

AVERY. You're very intuitive.

ELLIOT. Thanks?

AVERY. So how did you end up here alone?

ELLIOT. I came to see my girlfriend. I work out of town.

AVERY. You can't stay with her?

ELLIOT. I didn't actually tell her that I was coming. It was kind of a spur of the moment thing.

AVERY. *(sarcastically)* She sounds perfectly charming.

ELLIOT. You don't know anything about her.

AVERY. I'm assuming.

ELLIOT. You shouldn't make assumptions. It's rude.

AVERY. That's a defensive way to put it.

ELLIOT. I'm not defensive.

AVERY. You sure fooled me.

ELLIOT. She's very nice, okay. She has her moments, but I find her an overall enjoyable person. She doesn't make assumptions about others, and she most certainly does not barricade herself in strangers' bathrooms without warning.

AVERY. Slightly defensive.

ELLIOT. It's a fact.

AVERY. She doesn't know what she's missing. It's a wonderful way to meet new people.

ELLIOT. So you do this all the time?

AVERY. You can't do it all the time or it loses its appeal…

(There is a silence.)

That was a joke. I'm sorry. I have a horrible sense of humor. So…what do you do for a living?

ELLIOT. Nothing.

AVERY. You do nothing?

ELLIOT. Look, it doesn't really matter what I do. You're the one sitting in a hotel bathroom trying to make pleasant conversation. I have half a mind to call security.

AVERY. That's no way to talk to a girl.

ELLIOT. I'm not talking to a girl. I'm talking to a door.

AVERY. Maybe the door has feelings!

ELLIOT. You're insane!

AVERY. Well excuse me for trying to make small talk!

(They are both quiet.)

I'm sorry for that. I'm very touchy tonight.

ELLIOT. *(quietly)* I quit my job.

AVERY. What?

ELLIOT. *(He says it a bit louder now.)* I quit my job; last week, actually.

AVERY. What happened? You don't sound very pleased about the situation. Not that you should.

ELLIOT. It's silly. I really shouldn't have said anything. *(pause)* I was just unhappy. I got to the point where I felt like I was missing something, so I tried to make a change. I thought that if I quit maybe I wouldn't feel so bland.

AVERY. Did it work?

ELLIOT. No, I'm still just as stressed as I was before. It's more than just my job. It's everything. It's my life. Nothing is working out the way it's supposed to. I don't even know what I want. I'm going through my midlife crisis at twenty-six.

AVERY. Is that why you're here?

ELLIOT. Telling my life story to a faceless stranger?

AVERY. You know what I mean.

ELLIOT. I thought that if I just showed up here maybe we could work things out, go back to how we used to be. Me and my girlfriend, that is. It's been hard.

AVERY. Why is it that she's here and you're not?

ELLIOT. She had a big job opportunity here. It was only supposed to be temporary but...

AVERY. Then why are you trying to fix it?

ELLIOT. What?

AVERY. Why are you trying to fix something if it's not working? If it's not making you happy. I mean, it's kind of like…

(She thinks for a moment.)

…like a refrigerator. If after a while it's not working, you can try to fix it, but there might be a point where you just have to buy a new one. There's no point in keeping it around. Everything in it will eventually go bad. Does that make any sense?

ELLIOT. I can't buy a new life, though, and I certainly can't buy a new girlfriend.

AVERY. But you can start over. Like with your job. Just get a new…everything.

ELLIOT. Well that's dramatic, but it's an idea.

AVERY. I know a couple things about drama. It's kind of my specialty.

ELLIOT. Like what?

AVERY. Just little things.

ELLIOT. Yeah?

AVERY. My family is insane, like bat shit crazy, you know? I know everyone says that but mine is a special kind of crazy. My sister used to wait for the phone to ring at least three times before answering even if she was next to it. My mom was the worst, though. Everything in our house had to be nice and organized. She insisted that the toilet paper hang "over" because it was more appealing. I've never found toilet paper to be appealing. Little things like that drove me insane.

ELLIOT. So, when you ran in here tonight…?

AVERY. I don't know. It kind of just happened. Irene and I were sitting in a cafe on 83rd talking. I think at some point I started ranting about the froth in my drink and how much I hated the word "froth." It's just a strange word, if you've ever really looked at it. I prefer "foam"…So I finished my rant, eventually, and she was quiet for a little while. Then she turns to me and says,

"You're crazy sometimes, you know that?" As if it was nothing. As if she was saying, "You're wearing a yellow shirt today, you know that?" I was not wearing a yellow shirt, and I most certainly am not crazy. I mean, I never ate paste as a kid. That's got to count for something.

I may have overreacted a bit, said something about moving to another country, shaving my head, or something to shake her up a bit before I made a run for it. Irene followed me here. She can usually calm me down when I get worked up. Like I said, drama is my specialty.

ELLIOT. I'm sorry. I'd give you advice but I'm not really in the position to give any.

AVERY. It's okay, I feel better now. Talking about it helped more than advice would have. I can leave if you like. I think the bathroom has served its purpose.

ELLIOT. No, it's fine. You can stay if you want to.

(There is a light knocking on the hotel room door. After a moment the knocking becomes louder.)

AVERY. If it's Irene, tell her I jumped out the window.

*(**ELLIOT** walks to the door and opens it. He sees **JEN** on the other side and immediately shuts the door again.)*

AVERY. That works too.

ELLIOT. It's Jen. *(frantically)* You can't be here right now.

JEN. *(from hallway)* Elliot?

AVERY. I think the front door is a bit occupied at the moment, but I can make a run for it if you like.

ELLIOT. Now is not the time for humor. Hold on, is there a window in there?

AVERY. We're five stories up!

JEN. Elliot, open the door. This isn't funny.

ELLIOT. *(frantically, to **JEN**)* The place is a mess, hold on. *(quietly, to **AVERY**)* Just don't make any noise okay?

(pause)

Okay?

AVERY. Am I allowed to answer that?

ELLIOT. No. Just stay quiet.

*(***ELLIOT*** walks over to the door and opens it. **JEN** walks past him into the room. **ELLIOT** follows her, leaving the door ajar.)*

Sorry, I just wanted to clean a couple of things.

JEN. So you slam a door in my face?

ELLIOT. The place was a wreck.

JEN. You're staying at a bargain hotel. What did you expect? What was that on the phone, anyway?

ELLIOT. It was just some people from down the hall. It wasn't a problem.

JEN. Well it sounded like a problem. It sounded like a pretty big problem, actually. Then again you hung up on me. I came here expecting the Norman Conquest.

ELLIOT. How about I make it up to you? We can go around the corner and get some dinner.

*(***AVERY*** starts rummaging around the bathroom.)*

JEN. I already ate. I would have waited, but it was before you called. I'm really glad to see you though. How long are you here for?

ELLIOT. I'm not sure yet. Any word on when they'll be transferring you back?

JEN. I haven't really had a chance to ask. There's so much going on in the office with this new client we've got coming in.

*(***AVERY*** makes a bit of noise as she looks around. **JEN** looks towards the bathroom.)*

ELLIOT. How about going to get some coffee?

JEN. I'm not really in the mood to go anywhere. I had a pretty long day. Why don't we just stay in and catch up. You said you wanted to talk?

ELLIOT. Now probably isn't the best time.

JEN. It's as good of a time as any. After all, we've got this hotel room to ourselves tonight. If you're really not up for talking I can think of some other things –

(**AVERY** *purposely knocks something over.* **JEN** *looks over to the bathroom.*)

ELLIOT. You know what, that coffee sounds great.

JEN. What was that?

ELLIOT. Just…pipes. You know these old hotels. So about that coffee…

JEN. I said I wasn't in the mood. You know, maybe we should talk about this.

ELLIOT. Can't we talk later?

JEN. Why can't we talk now?

ELLIOT. It's complicated.

JEN. Complicated? We have a few problems, sure, but it's not "complicated."

ELLIOT. So now you'll admit that we have problems?

JEN. Why are you being like this?

ELLIOT. I'm really not in the mood to fight right now.

JEN. You asked me to come over.

ELLIOT. I know.

JEN. You said you wanted to talk things through.

ELLIOT. I know.

JEN. Then why are you avoiding it?

ELLIOT. I don't know.

JEN. This is so typical of you.

ELLIOT. It's compli –

JEN. Don't you dare say it's complicated.

ELLIOT. Can we go somewhere else for this?

JEN. Can you give me a straight answer?!

ELLIOT. There's a stranger in my bathroom!

JEN. Is everything a joke to you? Seriously, do you sit and think of ways to push my buttons, because that's what it feels like sometimes.

(The door is suddenly pushed open as **IRENE** *re-enters the room.)*

IRENE. Wow, you don't ever close your door, do you?

ELLIOT. I'm sorry. Do I know you? You must have the wrong room.

IRENE. You're joking right? I just ran four blocks. You could be insane. I mean, you look nice but –

*(***ELLIOT*** mouths a "no" behind* **JEN**'s *back.)*

IRENE. What are you doing? *(through the bathroom door)* Avery?

(There is a silence. Everybody looks at the bathroom door.)

AVERY. Yes.

JEN. Elliot, you better explain what is going on right now, because unless there is someone dying in your bathroom we are done. Do you hear me? Finished.

ELLIOT. I can't.

JEN. What do you mean, you can't? Did you hear what I just said?

ELLIOT. I can't because if I say it's complicated you'll just get angrier.

JEN. Elliot!

ELLIOT. I told you there was someone in my bathroom.

JEN. You never said it was a girl.

ELLIOT. What difference does that make?

JEN. Get her out of there!

ELLIOT. Jen –

JEN. Now!

ELLIOT. What do you expect me to do? I can't exactly break the door down.

JEN. Do something! Jesus, Elliot I don't care. Just fix this.

ELLIOT. What did you say?

JEN. I said fix this!

ELLIOT. Why fix it when it's not working?

JEN. Excuse me?

ELLIOT. Our relationship – I can't fix it. I've tried to but I can't anymore.

JEN. I don't see what that has to do with you hiding a girl in your bathroom.

ELLIOT. It has everything to do with that. I hardly see you anymore and half the time we're just fighting anyway. I'm sick of coming second to your job.

JEN. I am two seconds from walking out of this hotel.

ELLIOT. The problem isn't me, Jen.

JEN. What are you trying to say?

ELLIOT. I need to buy a new refrigerator.

JEN. Refrigerator?

ELLIOT. Maybe you should go.

JEN. Are you breaking up with me? You come all the way here and invite me over to break up with me?

ELLIOT. I don't know. I think so.

JEN. Well at least you were creative.

IRENE. …Well that's great. I'm just gonna…

(She walks between them to the bathroom door.)

ELLIOT. Jen, I'm sorry.

IRENE. Avery, I'm sorry.

JEN. Sorry doesn't even begin to cover this. Look, if this is really what you want then fine, but was the elaborate setup really necessary? You know what, don't answer that.

IRENE. *(to* **JEN***)* I think this is all just a really big misunderstanding.

JEN. Oh I bet you're enjoying this.

IRENE. *(to* **AVERY***)* You know what, forget I said anything. That bathroom sounds pretty nice. Do you mind if I take a look? Maybe climb out the window?

AVERY. We could always make a parachute out of the shower curtains.

JEN. She's crazy too? Wow, tonight is just full of surprises.

AVERY. You're one to talk.

IRENE. She's not crazy.

JEN. She's trying to turn a shower curtain into a science project.

AVERY. It's complicated.

JEN. Of course it is.

ELLIOT. Can we not have this discussion here?

JEN. That's fine. I can't do all this "complicated," Elliot. Call me when you work out your problems.

(*JEN walks out, slamming the door behind her.*)

AVERY. She sounds charming.

ELLIOT. That could have gone better.

IRENE. You compared her to a refrigerator.

AVERY. It was a metaphor.

IRENE. *(to AVERY)* Can you come out so we can talk about this?

AVERY. The refrigerator?

IRENE. Avery…

AVERY. You called me crazy.

IRENE. It was an "in the moment" thing. I only kind of meant it.

AVERY. I know. I kind of overreacted. I blame the froth. *(pause)* I'll be out in a minute.

IRENE. This seems way too easy.

ELLIOT. You're welcome.

IRENE. Oh. Nice job, Clark Kent. *(to AVERY)* I'll wait outside. *(to ELLIOT)* Try not to screw this one up.

(*IRENE walks out into the hallway.*)

AVERY. I guess I have to come out now.

ELLIOT. I guess so.

AVERY. This was really nice. Thank you.

ELLIOT. Are you going to come out or keep talking about how nice it was?

AVERY. Elliot, could you close your eyes?

ELLIOT. What for?

AVERY. I don't want to ruin the mystery. Not really knowing each other makes it feel daring.

ELLIOT. I don't really have a choice, do I?

AVERY. Where's your sense of adventure?

(He closes his eyes.)

ELLIOT. Okay, they're closed.

*(**AVERY** quietly opens the door and walks out into the main room. She walks over to the table and grabs a pen and paper. She quickly scribbles something down and walks back to where **ELLIOT** is standing.)*

AVERY. Keep 'em closed.

(She puts the piece of paper in his hand and kisses him lightly.)

Thank you.

(She rushes out of the room, closing the door behind her.)

ELLIOT. Avery?

*(**ELLIOT** walks over to the hotel room door. They are now standing on either side of it.)*

AVERY. Elliot?

ELLIOT. Does this mean I'll see you around?

AVERY. I don't know. Keep your door open.

(blackout)

CIRCUITS

by Rachel Lepore

CIRCUITS was presented in a staged reading as part of the Thespian Playworks program at the 2012 Thespian Festival on June 30. Carolyn Greer directed and Nicholas C. Pappas was the dramaturg.

EMILY .... Elaina Marie Faust
JACK ....Mickey Cole, Jr.
HUGH .... Ryan Kelly Gregory

ABOUT THE PLAYWRIGHT

Rachel Lepore is an actress and playwright from Las Vegas, NV. Currently, she is studying theatre at New York University at the Playwright's Horizons studio, where she is soaking up knowledge and devouring a copious number of knishes. *Circuits* is her first published play, and nothing has been more rewarding for her than working on it over the course of the Thespian Festival. She plans to keep writing plays, and hopes to one day be able to support herself through her theatre endeavors alone. In the meantime, she'd like to thank her friends and family for supporting her, Mr. Morris for believing in the strength of her writing, her original *Circuits* team for being the absolute best people in the world, and her family again, because they deserve that much love.

CHARACTERS

EMILY - Sixteen.

JACK - Her brother, nineteen.

HUGH - Emily's project partner, sixteen, a little bit geeky.

Scene 1

(Lights up on the room of a teenage girl. It is entirely free of clutter. A clean mirror sits near her closet door. Her desk has been carefully organized. At the desk sits **EMILY DANVERS**, *age sixteen. She's fiercely concentrating on what she is writing.* **EMILY** *is wearing a nice black dress with small black heels as she works. Against the back wall is her bed. It would have been neatly made were it not for the teenage boy laying down on it. This is* **EMILY**'s *brother,* **JACK**, *age nineteen. Unlike* **EMILY**, *he's dressed very casually. While lying down, he tosses a football up against the ceiling.* **EMILY** *ignores it for a while, before spinning her chair around.)*

EMILY. Can you please stop doing that?

JACK. Does it annoy you?

EMILY. Immensely.

JACK. Then no.

EMILY. Jack, you are insufferable.

JACK. Insufferable? Can't you just call me a pain in the ass?

EMILY. Does it annoy you?

JACK. A little.

EMILY. Then no.

*(***EMILY*** abruptly turns back to her work, and* **JACK** *returns to tossing the ball at the ceiling. This time, however, she manages to ignore it. Noticing this,* **JACK** *stops and sits up.)*

JACK. Whatcha doin'?

EMILY. I fail to see how it matters to you in any way, shape, or form.

JACK. Just tell me.

EMILY. Why should I?

JACK. *(whining)* Ems!

EMILY. *(mocking)* Jackie!

JACK. I'm just curious as to what you're up to. That's what big brothers are supposed to do, right?

EMILY. It's a project for my physics class, okay? I'm doing a rough draft of the essay portion.

JACK. Nice! Can I help?

EMILY. Jack, I hate to break it to you, but you barely passed physics with a D.

JACK. I'm still good with my hands though! What are you doing for the project?

EMILY. We're building a circuit. It's going to be a little robot. It'll move forward when we press a button or something. We haven't decided on all of the details yet.

JACK. We? This a group project or something?

EMILY. It's a partner project. I'm working with Hugh. He's a good partner to work with.

JACK. Do you like him?

EMILY. Look, I don't know him that well, okay? All I know is that he's pretty nice, and he's pretty smart.

JACK. Well, he must be if you're not whining about working with him.

EMILY. I don't whine, Jack.

JACK. Oh, really? "Jackie! I can't believe that she's making me do all of the work again! Ugh! Life is so, like, unfair."

EMILY. One, I sound nothing like that. Two, I will never, ever, even while being imitated, use the word "like" out of its proper context. Ever.

JACK. Jeez. So Hugh knows what he's doing with circuits?

EMILY. Yes. He's in the robotics club.

JACK. Explains the robot-themed circuit you got going there.

EMILY. It's fun.

JACK. You have an interesting definition of fun. But hey, whatever you nerds do.

(After taking a glance at the digital clock on her desk, EMILY abruptly stands and walks toward the door.)

Whoa! Where's the fire?

EMILY. I'm leaving.

JACK. Are you actually offended, because I called you a nerd?

EMILY. No. Mom said to be ready to leave by noon. It's 11:45.

JACK. Where are you headed?

EMILY. Jack, today is your funeral.

JACK. Oh.

EMILY. Did you really forget?

JACK. Um, yeah. Seems like it slipped my mind. That's pretty pathetic, huh?

EMILY. I'm not surprised.

JACK. Well, that explains all the black you have on.

EMILY. If you're done, I'd like to go.

JACK. Wait!

EMILY. Yes?

JACK. Do you – do you know if they managed to fix up my body? I mean, there was a lot of glass, and bl –

EMILY. You look fine Jack. It's like you fell asleep.

JACK. Good. 'Cause I'd like to think of myself as a pretty handsome guy, and that corpse? Not handsome.

EMILY. It's nice to see that being dead hasn't stopped you from being an idiot.

JACK. Hey! I'm right though, right?

EMILY. Go to hell, Jack.

(She exits. A beat.)

JACK. That isn't funny anymore!

(lights down)

Scene 2

(Lights up on the bedroom. **JACK** *lies sprawled across the bed, tossing the football up into the air again and again. His outfit has not changed. After a few moments,* **EMILY** *enters in her pajamas, but with her hair brushed and her makeup already done. She freezes upon seeing him on the bed.)*

EMILY. Didn't you leave?

JACK. Nope.

EMILY. Then, where did you go last night?

JACK. Closet. It's more comfortable than the floor. Don't know why I didn't try it earlier.

*(***EMILY*** growls in displeasure as she tries to contain her anger. She crosses over to her mirror and begins to French braid her hair.)*

JACK. French braids? Are you really that angry?

EMILY. What are you talking about?

JACK. Ever since you learned how to do that stupid hairstyle, you use it when you're angry.

EMILY. It's not stupid!

JACK. It makes you look like you're twelve, Ems.

EMILY. Fine! I won't do it.

*(***EMILY*** begins to undo the braid she was working on, then growls and starts redoing it again.)*

EMILY. Forget it! I'm just going do my hair like this. It's dirty anyway.

JACK. Someone's in a bad mood this morning.

EMILY. Well, I got my hopes up thinking that you were gone. Sorry for being a bit upset.

JACK. I'm back from the dead! Aren't you happy?

EMILY. Frankly, no.

JACK. Why not?

EMILY. Because I'm not crazy!

JACK. Uh, Ems? Nobody said that you were.

EMILY. But I have to be. I mean, it's not like you could be real!

JACK. Um, ouch.

EMILY. Well, sorry if it hurts your feelings, but it's true. People don't just come back from the dead!

JACK. I have. I'm like a ghost or something, right?

EMILY. Wrong. You're like a, stress—or mental illness—induced hallucination, or something. Which is why I'm obviously crazy. Needs Medication Crazy.

JACK. Can you stop saying that I'm not real?

EMILY. Why should I? You're not real. Everything you do is in my head! You just act in the way that I expect you to. It's not like you could surp –

(JACK *cuts her off, jumping to his feet and looming over her.* EMILY *shrinks back, leaning against her mirror.*)

JACK. Stop it! Dammit! Just stop saying that!

EMILY. Jack, calm down!

JACK. I don't want you to be crazy, either! 'Cause you know what? If you're crazy, then you're right! I'm not real. You know what that means? It means that I'm dead. Dead dead.

EMILY. Jackie, I'm sorry, I didn't – I mean –

JACK. I don't wanna be dead dead, Ems. I don't. Don't make me.

(*There is an awkward pause. After a moment, still upset,* JACK *moves back to the bed and resumes tossing the football at the ceiling.* EMILY *turns to look in the mirror and smiles very softly.*)

EMILY. You have a reflection. That's a good sign, I guess.

JACK. Fantastic.

(*There is another bit of awkward silence.* EMILY *crosses to her drawers and pulls out a shirt. She then takes out a pair of pants from her closet.*)

EMILY. I'm sorry, Jackie.

(**EMILY** *exits.* **JACK** *lays across the bed and stops tossing the ball, holding it close to his chest. After a moment of thought, he angrily throws it down on the floor.*)

JACK. I won't die.

(lights down)

Scene 3

(JACK is still lying on the bed, though he now seems to be sleeping on it. EMILY enters in a rush, uncharacteristically tossing her backpack on the floor near her desk. Spotting the football on the floor, she tosses it at JACK's head.)

JACK. *(without opening his eyes yet)* You could've just asked me to get up.

EMILY. Rest in the closet.

JACK. *(sitting up)* Why should I?

EMILY. Because I have company coming over. Actually, better idea: Go to your own room.

JACK. I can't.

EMILY. Why not? You love annoying me too much?

JACK. Yes, but no. I'm not saying that I won't, Ems. I can't.

EMILY. Why not?

JACK. I don't know! I mean, I'd like to get a change of scenery too, but apparently being dead has rules and stuff.

EMILY. "Rules and stuff"? You are so painfully ineloquent.

JACK. That's nice to hear from you. Thanks.

EMILY. You're welcome. Now get in the closet! Please?

JACK. Why does it matter? Nobody else can see me!

EMILY. Really?

JACK. Yeah.

EMILY. I didn't know that.

JACK. Ah well. Whatcha gonna do? At least my cute little sister can see me!

EMILY. Fan-freaking-tastic. Well, I still want you in the closet. You can't distract me while I'm working!

JACK. And how would I do that?

EMILY. Oh, I'm sure that you and I both can think of a multitude of ways for you to drive me crazy.

JACK. Who's coming over, anyway? Howard?

EMILY. Hugh.

JACK. I knew that.

EMILY. Oh, I'm sure.

JACK. So when is he gonna get here?

EMILY. Soon.

JACK. How soon is soon?

EMILY. He said that he was grabbing some stuff from his house, and then he'd come right over. Mom's just going to send him up.

JACK. Does he live close?

EMILY. Moderately?

JACK. Does that mean he can drive?

EMILY. Yes, Jack. He can drive. He has his own car, too.

JACK. Well I'm not so sure you should be associating with a boy with a car. They're hooligans.

EMILY. Did you really just say, "hooligans"?

JACK. Yes. That's how deadly serious I am.

EMILY. Deadly. Hah. Now why are you pretending that you care?

JACK. I'm stalling for time until he gets here.

EMILY. Jack? Closet. Now.

JACK. *(whining)* Ems!

EMILY. *(mocking him)* Jackie!

(A knock is heard on the door.)

HUGH. Um, Emily? Is this your room? I'm gonna feel so stupid if this is the linen closet.

*(**EMILY** jumps and immediately pulls **JACK** off the bed. He stumbles forward, almost falling face-first on the floor, not having expected that.)*

JACK. Are you trying to kill me or something?

*(There is a pause as **EMILY** stares at him, and **JACK** registers what he said.)*

JACK. Sorry.

EMILY. Whatever. Just get in the closet. Now!

(As JACK enters the closet and closes the door, HUGH knocks on the door one last time.)

HUGH. Okay. If you're Emily, say so. If you're a pile of towels, remain silent.

EMILY. No, it's me! Sorry!

(EMILY rushes over to the door and opens it, ushering HUGH in. HUGH JONES is also sixteen and gives off a feeling of mild awkwardness as he moves, never quite standing straight up. Despite the geeky exterior, though, he remains decently attractive. He carries a bag with him, filled with papers and materials for their circuit project.)

EMILY. Sorry about that. I accidentally fell asleep.

HUGH. For ten minutes?

EMILY. It's just been a little hard for me to sleep at night.

HUGH. Oh. Sorry.

EMILY. It's nothing! Don't worry.

(HUGH sits down on the bed, accidentally sitting on the football. He takes it out from under him, looking at it.)

HUGH. Didn't take you for the sporty type, Emily.

EMILY. Believe me, I'm not. That's, ah, that's my brother's.

(HUGH drops it immediately, realizes that that's not a good thing to do to the memento, picks it back up, and carefully sets it down on the bed.)

HUGH. Sorry. Again.

EMILY. Don't worry about it. He has three more in his room still. Besides, it's not like they're fragile.

HUGH. He was on the football team at school, right?

EMILY. Quarterback. He was also going to play in college. Scholarship.

HUGH. It's...it's a shame, about the accident.

EMILY. He was driving drunk. I – it's...Can we just start working on the project?

HUGH. Y – yeah! Of course!

(**HUGH** *slides off of the bed and onto the floor. He opens up the bag and takes out a folder, as well as several parts for the circuit.*)

HUGH. I borrowed some pieces from the robotics club room. I figured that they wouldn't mind, so long as most of the bits go back after the project is done.

EMILY. All right. You're going to have to walk me through this, though.

(**EMILY** *and* **HUGH** *both reach for the papers at the same time. Their hands touch, and both freeze. They awkwardly withdraw their hands.*)

My circuitry knowledge is limited to making a light bulb go on and off.

HUGH. Oh, no worries. It's easy!

EMILY. Says the member of the robotics club.

HUGH. Says the Treasurer of the robotics club.

EMILY. Oh, well excuse me. I wasn't aware that I was speaking to someone of such a high title.

HUGH. Well, I think that I can forgive you this time.

EMILY. Phew. And there I was thinking that I was a goner.

HUGH. A goner?

EMILY. Yep. I'd be walking home one night, all alone, and suddenly I'd be jumped by an attack bot! There would be an epic battle, but I would obviously be no match for your creation. As my world would start to fade to black, I would just hear an echoing voice go, "You shouldn't have crossed the Treasurer!"

(*There is a pause.* **HUGH** *has never seen this playful side of* **EMILY** *before.* **EMILY** *begins to sink with the silence. She nervously chuckles.*)

EMILY. Ah, sorry if that was, you know, weird.

HUGH. No! Well, I mean, it was a little weird – but in a good way! I just wasn't expecting that from you. I didn't know that you were so funny.

EMILY. Oh, so is that why you didn't laugh?

HUGH. I was in shock, alright? You're not like that at school.

EMILY. Well, going to school has just been a bit hard lately.

HUGH. Sorry.

EMILY. You don't need to keep apologizing.

HUGH. Sor – mmm. It's just kind of awkward. How are you supposed to act when someone's died, anyway?

EMILY. I don't know. I just wish it wasn't like this. It's not going to kill me if somebody says his name, or mentions that he died, or even says that it was his fault.

HUGH. You're pretty strong.

EMILY. You really think so?

HUGH. Yeah. For sure.

EMILY. Thanks.

(There is another pause, but it is awkward for a different reason. EMILY breaks it with a cough.)

Well, we better get to work. So, Mr. Treasurer, how do you build a forward-moving robot?

HUGH. Well, I have a few papers here.

(HUGH removes several sheets of graph paper from the folder he brought with him.)

I made a few different sketches. I figured I'd see which one you like best.

(EMILY picks up one of the schematics and hands it to him. He glances it over. As he explains things, he points to them.)

HUGH. Okay, this one's probably the most complicated.

EMILY. Showoff.

HUGH. I thought it'd be cool! This one would move forward, backward, and in circles. See, this would pick up signals from our remote, and they'd go through this wire here to – this is really complicated, isn't it?

EMILY. The task was to design a *simple* circuit.

HUGH. Okay. So, next one.

(EMILY *takes the paper and hands it to him.* HUGH *looks it over again, shaking his head.*)

HUGH. Maybe we should skip to the last one?

EMILY. What's wrong with this one?

HUGH. It's wrong.

EMILY. Meaning?

HUGH. Meaning that I drafted it at two in the morning.

EMILY. So, is this circuit not salvageable?

HUGH. It might be better to just use the last one. I mean, this one could be fixed, but...

EMILY. You'd rather not?

HUGH. Yeah.

EMILY. All right.

(EMILY *looks down and moves to grab the last paper. This time,* HUGH *grabs her hand on purpose. They freeze again.*)

EMILY. Oh, so –

HUGH. Can I kiss you right now?

(As HUGH *and* EMILY *lean in,* JACK *shoves open the closet door and emerges, shutting it roughly behind him.* HUGH *does not notice.*)

JACK. Absolutely not.

(EMILY *jumps, looking over* HUGH*'s shoulder at* JACK *in surprise.*)

EMILY. What?

HUGH. Ah, I know that sounds weird. It's just, I've always kind of liked you, and it just seemed right.

JACK. Tell him to leave.

HUGH. If you don't want to, I get it, but if you do...

JACK. Now!

EMILY. No!

HUGH. Okay. Sorry. I didn't mean to upset you. That was creepy.

EMILY. No, it's not –

JACK. Make him leave, Emily!

HUGH. *(simultaneously)* It's not...?

EMILY. *(to* **JACK***)* Go away. Just leave me alone!

(**HUGH** *backs up slowly, grabbing his bag.*)

HUGH. I'm so sorry, Emily. I – I didn't mean to make you mad.

JACK. *(to* **HUGH***, who can't hear)* Leave us alone!

EMILY. Stop it!

HUGH. I – sorry. I'll – I'll leave.

(*In a flurry,* **HUGH** *exits.* **EMILY***, realizing the misunderstanding a beat too late, tries to run out to catch him. She fails and comes back, steaming.*)

EMILY. What the hell was that about?!

JACK. He wasn't going to kiss you while I'm here!

EMILY. Why not?

JACK. I don't wanna watch that!

EMILY. Then you should've shut the door!

JACK. Well I haven't approved of him!

EMILY. You sound ridiculous!

JACK. I'm just being your brother!

EMILY. You're dead! You don't get to approve of anyone!

JACK. Well I'm still here right now, so I do!

EMILY. No! I'm allowed to move on without you ruining everything!

JACK. So now I ruin everything?

EMILY. Um, yeah. You just ruined what could have been a great relationship, and you caused your own death!

JACK. Why the hell are you telling people that?

EMILY. Hmm, because it's true?

JACK. It's not!

EMILY. Jack, you went to a party that night and drove home at two in the morning. Your blood alcohol level was through the roof, and they found pot in your car. It was your own damn fault.

JACK. That is a horrible thing to tell someone.

EMILY. Oh? What do you want me to say then, huh? That the light pole jumped out at you? You killed yourself, whether you like it or not. Do you want me to lie about that?

JACK. No.

EMILY. Then what do you want?

JACK. I don't know! I hate this.

EMILY. Well, so do I.

JACK. You think you'd be happy that I'm around.

EMILY. Why?

JACK. Because you can still talk to me.

EMILY. Jack, you don't talk to me.

JACK. Oh?

EMILY. You just annoy me, and you mess up the good parts of my life. After all, it wasn't enough for you to mess up just your own.

JACK. Shut up, Emily.

EMILY. Why don't you shut up? You're not even supposed to be here!

JACK. Fine then. I'll leave!

EMILY. Good!

(JACK *attempts to exit through the door of* **EMILY***'s room, but an unseen wall stops him. He growls and retreats into the closet, slamming the door behind him.* **EMILY** *fights for something to yell out after him, but fails. Frustrated, she takes the football off of her bed and throws it violently to the ground. Noticing the papers still on the floor, she picks them up and brings them to her desk. Carefully, she sets them inside one of her drawers. Before she closes it, however, she takes the last one out. The lights fade as she sits at her desk and pores over it, trying to understand it.*)

Scene 4

(Lights up on the room, the next day. The room is oddly
empty. The football still lies where it was tossed the floor.
After a few moments of silence, **EMILY** *enters the room.*
She tosses her backpack where it was the other day.
Glancing around, she notices that **JACK** *isn't around.*
With a sigh, she opens the closet door.)

EMILY. Quit moping, Jackie. Jack?

*(***EMILY*** goes into the closet. She reemerges a few moments*
later, helping **JACK** *walk. He looks tired and pale,*
shaking with weakness. She moves him to the bed and
helps him sit down.)

Jack, are you all right? What happened?

JACK. I don't know. Beats me.

EMILY. You look terrible! What happened when you went
in there? You didn't come out all night.

JACK. I figured you were angry at me.

EMILY. Well, I was. That's not important right now. You
look...

JACK. Like a dead person?

EMILY. For lack of a better word, yes.

JACK. I don't know why. I feel like crap. All I did was rest.

EMILY. The entire time?

JACK. Yeah, I guess. I didn't realize how long it's been. Hey,
how long has it been?

EMILY. Almost twenty-four hours.

JACK. It's not like sleeping, Ems. It's kind of just like,
closing your eyes and floating away. It's nice. Or at
least, it was nice.

EMILY. You get nightmares?

JACK. Yeah.

EMILY. Seriously? You weren't even really sleeping.

JACK. So? It was still horrible. Everything was spinning.
I couldn't see. There were a lot of blurred lights. It

felt like I was going too fast. Then out of nowhere, everything stopped. I flung forward. My chest hurt, and my face felt like it was in a thorn bush, and then I fell. I was just lying there when you came into get me.

EMILY. Jack...do you know what that sounds like?

(JACK *takes a moment before the realization hits.*)

JACK. Think so?

EMILY. Definitely.

JACK. Why do I hurt so much though, Ems? I feel like I'm dead dead. I never felt like that before, Ems.

EMILY. Well, it happened after you rested, right?

JACK. Yeah. So?

EMILY. So maybe your body is trying to rest in peace, and you won't let it.

JACK. I don't wanna leave. I don't wanna be dead!

EMILY. It's too late for that!

JACK. I'm still here, so it's not too late!

EMILY. Why are you still here, Jack? Why don't you leave?

JACK. You're here! You can still see me, so I have a reason to stay.

EMILY. Jack! Listen to me. You died. It doesn't matter if it was your fault or not, or if you like it or not. You can't change what happened. It doesn't matter that you're here right now, because you still don't exist for anyone except me. You're sick like this.

JACK. (*weakly pushing himself off of the bed and stumbling toward the mirror*) I'm fine now. I just needed to sit for a minute.

EMILY. Liar.

(JACK *stands in front of the mirror. A look of revulsion crosses his face.*)

JACK. I thought you said that my reflection was normal!

(EMILY *moves toward the mirror, standing next to him.*)

EMILY. It is.

JACK. No. No it's not! It's gross! Ugh!

(JACK *pulls his arm back with the intention to smash the mirror to escape the image.* EMILY *reacts quickly enough to grab a hold of his arm and stop him.*)

EMILY. Jack!

(JACK *turns around, shaking his head, and returns to the bed. He covers his face in his hands, muttering to himself.* EMILY *goes after him.*)

EMILY. Jack! What did you see in there?

JACK. Decay, and cuts, and bugs, and –

EMILY. I didn't see any of that!

JACK. That's what I must look like right now.

EMILY. Quit being stubborn! If this is how you feel after being around for a few days, imagine how it'll feel after months? Years? You'd rather just be dead than feel like this, wouldn't you?

JACK. No. I know how this feels. I can handle this, no matter how bad it is. I don't know what death's like.

EMILY. Jack, that's –

JACK. Stupid. I know.

EMILY. It's not stupid, Jack.

JACK. Sure it is. I'm a coward.

EMILY. Being afraid doesn't make you a coward.

JACK. No?

EMILY. No, dummy.

(*There is a moment of silence as* JACK *thinks.* EMILY *sits next to him.*)

JACK. Did you ever look up to me? I just...I always wondered if you ever looked up to me. Ever.

EMILY. Of course I did!

JACK. Really?

EMILY. Yeah. I mean, it's true that you're an idiot, but... people like you. A lot. Your funeral had the entire high school and a good deal of your college at it, you know. That many people wouldn't show up if I was the one who died. Plus you were always athletic, and…I was jealous of those sorts of things.

JACK. You're kidding me.

EMILY. I'm not! It's true.

JACK. Thanks.

EMILY. I love you, Jack. I yell a lot, but I love you.

JACK. I love you too, Ems. I always will, too.

EMILY. Same.

(*JACK places an arm around* **EMILY**. *After a second,* **EMILY** *hugs him, burying her face in his chest, and begins to quietly sob.*)

JACK. Are you – are you actually crying?

EMILY. Shut up.

JACK. You haven't cried once this entire time.

EMILY. I told you to shut up.

(*JACK complies, gently holding her. Before* **EMILY** *can finish crying, a knock is heard at the door.*)

HUGH. Emily? Please let me in. I know for sure now that this isn't a linen closet. So, you know, don't pretend to be a towel.

(**EMILY** *quickly sits up and wipes her tears away. She and* JACK *exchange a look before she stands up.*)

EMILY. Sorry! I was sleeping!

(**EMILY** *opens the door for him. He enters, nervous.*)

HUGH. Sorry to burst in and ruin your nap, again. I realized that I left some stuff here.

EMILY. Yeah, the papers. I was looking over them the other night, and I think that we should use that third design for the project.

HUGH. You still want to work with me?

EMILY. Yeah. Look, Hugh, I'm not angry at you or anything.

HUGH. Really? I mean, if you are, you don't have to say that you're not. I was out of line, and it was kind of creepy, and –

EMILY. No, no! It wasn't creepy. I shouldn't have flipped out.

HUGH. Still, I shouldn't have done that.

EMILY. It's okay. I mean, if I hadn't been so crazy at the time, I think I would have let you. So, I'm sorry.

HUGH. Me too.

(There is an awkward pause. A sudden thought hits EMILY.*)*

EMILY. What were you planning on doing if I did hate you and never wanted to see you again?

HUGH. Grab the papers from here, run, and build the thing at home. Then I'd let you take equal credit.

EMILY. That's nice. Well, you don't need to do that now! When should we meet up to actually build the circuit and everything?

HUGH. Well, we can meet during lunch in the club room. Mr. Brenner won't mind.

EMILY. All right. Sounds good to me.

HUGH. Yeah.

(There is another awkward pause. Out of nowhere, HUGH *suddenly speaks.)*

Will you go on a date with me?

EMILY. H – huh?

HUGH. Sorry. Awkward.

EMILY. No, not awkward. Just...sudden.

HUGH. It's just, you said that you would've kissed me, and I still like you, so I figured...I figured that, maybe it's a little weird to try and kiss you so soon, but if we went on a date or two, it wouldn't be so strange.

*(*EMILY *apprehensively glances toward* JACK, *who has been observing the entire time. He nods, and she beams.)*

EMILY. That actually sounds pretty nice, Hugh. So, when should we go out?

HUGH. Well, how about a movie on Saturday?

EMILY. Works for me.

HUGH. I agree! Well, ah, that should be great.

(*There is another awkward pause. This time, it makes* **EMILY** *laugh a little.*)

I–I should probably be going now. Let you get back to your nap.

EMILY. Thanks, Hugh. See you at school? No more hiding from me?

HUGH. Yeah. We have the project to work on.

EMILY. And outside of the project?

HUGH. Definitely.

JACK. Just hug him already.

(*Just as* **HUGH** *moves to exit,* **EMILY** *catches him in a hug. He freezes, surprised for a moment, before he hugs her back. She lets go and he follows suit.*)

EMILY. Good bye, Hugh.

HUGH. Bye, Ems. Hey, is it okay if I call you Ems?

EMILY. (*pauses before smiling*) Yeah. I like it.

HUGH. Okay. Bye!

(*Grinning wildly,* **HUGH** *leaves.*)

JACK. I'm gonna miss you, Ems.

EMILY. You're going to leave?

JACK. I'm dead. It's about time I move on and act like it.

EMILY. You're brave.

JACK. Nah.

EMILY. I'll miss you too. How are you going to move on, though? How does it work?

JACK. I think that I just need to rest some more. Only really let go this time.

EMILY. Can I lie down with you? Kind of like when we were little?

(**JACK** *pauses, thinks about it, and then laughs.*)

JACK. Sure.

EMILY. What was so funny?

JACK. Nothing. I'm just glad we're getting along.

> (**EMILY** *nods and smiles. After a second, they both lie down. As they fall asleep, a light shines on the bed. It grows brighter and brighter until, abruptly, all of the lights go out. When they slowly come on a moment later,* **JACK** *is gone.* **EMILY** *is alone. She stirs for a brief moment and, noticing* **JACK***'s absence, smiles softly and grabs his football, holding it tight, before going back to sleep. The lights go down again.)*

End of play

SOUTH OF SOMEPLACE

by I.B. Hopkins

SOUTH OF SOMEPLACE was presented in a staged reading as part of the Thespian Playworks program at the 2012 Thespian Festival on June 30. Michael Daehn directed and Mark D. Kaufmann was the dramaturg.

OPAL... Cass Neumann
ROMAN ....Justin Whipple
VESS..Kaitlyn Noble
CAMPBELL..Drew Brown
INDIA ROSE... Sarah Bubbers
TESS...Adriana Luffman
JOLENE...Katy Nelson
SEYMOUR ....Michael Cienfuegos-Baca

ABOUT THE PLAYWRIGHT

I.B. Hopkins is a native of Gainesville, Georgia. He is the youngest son of Marsha and Benjie Hopkins and is sibling to Boone, Mayes, and Ethan Hopkins. Isaac graduated from Gainesville High School in the spring of 2012, and he plans to pursue the arts of writing and of theatre in college and beyond. In addition to this play and *The Goatman Cometh*, a 2011 Playworks finalist, he has authored numerous other plays and musicals with an emphasis on the 21st-century American South.

CHARACTERS

OPAL HARGROVE FAIRFIELD - Early middle-aged, all lipstick and pearls.

ROMAN S. FAIRFIELD - Eighteen, frustrated, with a stern nose.

VESS GREENE JOHNSTON - A stately would-be matron with all the glamour of a peacock.

CAMPBELL JOHNSTON - A middle-aged man, used to his wife.

INDIA ROSE JOHNSTON - A teenager, younger than Roman. She embodies a strikingly lovely simplicity. Campbell and Vess's daughter.

TESS GREENE UNDERWOOD - An early middle-aged woman with the persona of a faded magnolia. Vess's sister.

JOLENE UNDERWOOD - Tess's daughter...bless her heart.

SEYMOUR - An ethereal elderly man, an undeniable presence in the Fairfield home.

SETTING

Now, though hardly recognizable. Out from Atlanta. The place is insulated, tucked far away from the outside world in the decaying rear garden of a once-elegant Southern home.

(Light opens on a place that belongs to dinosaurs: the antiquated, unkempt rear garden of a Southern home that still clings to traces of a bygone grandeur. Doors upstage lead into the house; paths downstage trail off to the grounds. The sounds of prehistory – bullfrogs, cicadas, circling mosquitoes, a screen door slamming, leaves rustling as birds flit among their shade – fill the space.)

(SEYMOUR, a man of some age, enters the garden, paces for a few moments, and feels his unique depression on the earth beneath each step. Before he can admire the foliage too long, ROMAN S. FAIRFIELD clomps onstage with staccato strides. He rips a leaf from some over-grown vegetation; he tears it into smaller leaves. SEYMOUR watches intently and approaches the boy without being noticed. A pause. OPAL FAIRFEILD enters from the house with a tray of coffee fixings, rippling the equilibrium. She wears proud albeit dated pearls over skin thin with years of worry.)

OPAL. Roman! Oh, there you are. What are you doing out here?

ROMAN. Nothing. What are you doing?

OPAL. Just thought they might like a cup of coffee when they get here. And actually I'm fixing to go finish getting myself ready.

ROMAN. You look fine.

OPAL. Oh! That's sweet of you, honey…I told DeLois it would never hold in this heat, but I guess I'll just have to make do…

ROMAN. When're they coming?

OPAL. *(a little strained)* I'm expecting folks any minute.

ROMAN. He didn't seem real excited about them coming – wouldn't say a word to me when I took him his pills this morning.

OPAL. Well, you can't take that personally. *(grasping for something more manageable)* Oh, Roman! I told you two weeks ago to cut some of this kudzu down. Gracious, I spent the whole weekend cleaning up inside because I thought you'd taken care of things out here. It looks like a perfect sty – like not a soul lives here at all.

ROMAN. Sorry. I didn't really have the time.

OPAL. Lord-have-mercy, son. You're just as stubborn as your – as a mule.

*(**ROMAN**'s eyes dart as though bored.)*

ROMAN. It sure is hot today. It's felt like summer since middle of April.

OPAL. Roman…

ROMAN. What?

OPAL. Roman, I hate to have to bring this up, but I want to make sure that you know exactly what your responsibilities are today. It may –

ROMAN. Mom, I know –

OPAL. Please, just listen to me. It may seem odd to you; it may seem ridiculous, but you have got to pay close attention while they're here. This could well be the most important couple of days of your life, and it will – God willing – determine how the rest of it plays out. I'm not having you discount it all.

ROMAN. But I don't see what the big –

OPAL. Exactly. You don't see, but just trust that I do. Please. *(choosing her words)* You have got to be careful around them.

ROMAN. *(a teenaged stone)* Fine, I will.

OPAL. Because every word you say, every step you take will be scru –

ROMAN. I say I will.

OPAL. Now do you want to come on inside and help me finish getting the house ready?

ROMAN. Not really.

(A small bell tinkles from above.)

OPAL. Well, go ahead. The Colonel won't wait. And put your tie on while you're up there. You don't have a sport coat that still fits, do you?

ROMAN. No, I outgrew them all. And can't you go?

OPAL. Roman, they're going to be here any minute, and I still need to go put my face on. I know they're going to think I have just lost my ever-lovin' mind having company and me looking like this...

(The small bell rings again – more impatient this time.)

OPAL. *(gesturing to the upper window)* Roman.

ROMAN. I can wait for them out here.

OPAL. I know he can be difficult sometimes, but –

*(The bell rings a third time, edged with impatience. **OPAL** stares long at **ROMAN** before exiting back into the house. **ROMAN** paces; **SEYMOUR** breaks his silence.)*

*(**SEYMOUR** comes into view. He goes unnoticed and yet is himself interested in **ROMAN**.)*

SEYMOUR. Oh, how children laugh in early summer – before it grows too warm. Laugh and love and forget their toil. Perfect songbirds in a flowering tree.

ROMAN. *(No notice taken of **SEYMOUR**, he addresses the Colonel's window above.)* Damn you.

*(**ROMAN** has not noticed the dining-room-chair-stiff figures nearing behind him. These erect spines belong to **VESS** and **CAMPBELL JOHNSTON**. The two glide into the garden; they then proceed to vulture down upon **ROMAN**.)*

VESS. Hello there, Roman.

*(A third form, **INDIA ROSE JOHNSTON**, enters the garden as if freshly birthed. She is simplicity, and she is beauty.)*

ROMAN. Hello?

VESS. *(forcing herself forward)* Oh, it is you. I hadn't seen you in so long; I wouldn't have known you in a crowd!

CAMPBELL. Give the boy some room to breathe, now. He probably doesn't recognize us either. I bet you've scared him half to death.

VESS. Oh, it can't have been all that long since we saw each other…

CAMPBELL. Well, let's see now: Roman would have been about…

ROMAN. I was six.

VESS. See. He does remember his Auntie Vess and Uncle Campbell.

CAMPBELL. *(urging his daughter forward)* And, of course, he knows our little India Rose. The two of you used to love playing together when you were small.

(INDIA ROSE fiddles with her hair.)

INDIA ROSE. It's good to see you again.

ROMAN. Hi.

INDIA ROSE. Hi.

(beat)

VESS. Oh, Roman, we do hate to be here under such unfortunate circumstances. It seems like the only time I ever do get around to visiting the ones I love is when something tragic happens.

ROMAN. Maybe you're bad luck.

VESS. Pardon?

ROMAN. It's good to see y'all.

VESS. Isn't it though?

ROMAN. Yeah. I'll, uh, just go tell Opal you're here.

CAMPBELL. I'm sorry?

VESS. You call your mother by her Christian name?! When did that start?

ROMAN. Well, she calls me Roman.

VESS. Oh, dear me.

CAMPBELL. Do go on and tell her we're here, please, Roman.

*(**ROMAN** retreats into the house, back into mute collusion, one eye carefully trained on **INDIA ROSE**.)*

VESS. *(a little too loudly)* Oh, I can't wait to see that dear, dear woman. It has been too, too long...*(**ROMAN** shuts the door behind him.)* Can you believe the nerve of that cantankerous boy?! Just like the Colonel. *(reviewing the overgrown vegetation)* I don't know how they can stand to let this place go all to ruin like they have. You can hardly see the house for the vines grown up the side. Guess they'll be leaving soon enough, though...no reason to stay.

CAMPBELL. So long as we get what's ours...

VESS. We've just got to be careful.

CAMPBELL. Do you think she's here yet?

VESS. It is irrelevant whether or not my sister shows her ugly little head at all. Somewhere in that...misguided heart of hers she knows what's right. She's not going to be a problem.

CAMPBELL. But she will be here...

VESS. Oh, to be sure. With that chalky-faced, ill-mannered child of hers in tow, no doubt.

CAMPBELL. How could anyone look at that pointy little creature next to our India Rose?

INDIA ROSE. Daddy, I don't –

CAMPBELL. That's my girl. I know you'll make us proud.

*(They share concreted silence while **VESS**'s gaze is fixed on the Colonel's window.)*

VESS. All right now, we'd better hurry. We must have a chance to look in on the Colonel while he's still seeing folks.

CAMPBELL. Well, I'll go up, but I'm not letting him lay a finger on me. Those "manshakes" of his are pure sadism.

VESS. He's breathing through a tube, honey. I think you'll be fine.

INDIA ROSE. I think I remember playing in this garden when I was little.

VESS. Really? Well, do you recall a boy?

INDIA ROSE. I think so…and another girl, too.

(Toting **ROMAN** *along behind,* **OPAL** *re-enters the garden from the house in grand style.* **OPAL***'s arms are spread generously to the famished guests.)*

OPAL. Oh, Vess! Campbell! It's been so, so long. Too long.

VESS. Well, you know, we hate for it to be under such tragic circumstances…

OPAL. *(fraying)* Yes. We do what we have to do, but I do appreciate y'all coming. *(slathering her smile on again)* Now we're going to stop all this dreariness this instant. No one is dead just yet so we're going to celebrate being alive and together with good friends while we have the time.

CAMPBELL. You're too right. There's no sense in mourning the living.

OPAL. Exactly.

(CAMPBELL *embraces the infectious spirit as his words crawl up into the corners of his mouth.)*

CAMPBELL. It's wonderful to see you, Opal. You look great.

OPAL. Campbell Johnston, you charmer, that smile of yours should have been outlawed years ago! I do, don't I? *(a beat)* Oh, my word, my word! Is that y'all's little girl?! Could that be y'all's sweet little India Rose over there?

INDIA ROSE. *(bashfully)* Yes, ma'am. It's me.

OPAL. She's just a vision. You must be so, so proud.

VESS. Why, thank you. India, tell your Auntie Opal "thank you."

INDIA ROSE. Thank you.

VESS. And we hardly recognized your Roman earlier. He sure has grown up fast.

OPAL. It seems like every time I turn my head he's grown another foot.

ROMAN. I've still only got two.

CAMPBELL. And you know, he's really favoring Edgar now.

VESS. It's like he were standing here with us.

OPAL. *(Her words sticking in her larynx like peanut butter – the crunchy kind.)* Yes…I…Thank you.

CAMPBELL. So…do you know when are the others arriving?

OPAL. *(calm betrayal)* Any time now. Y'all're the first, but I'm sure they'll be here soon. Did Roman offer y'all some coffee?

VESS. He certainly did. Opal, you've raised a perfect gentleman. We were just so excited about seeing y'all that we hadn't fixed a cup yet.

OPAL. Oh, Vess. You're going to make me blush. *(taking her time to smile toothily at* **INDIA ROSE** *and* **ROMAN***)* Umm…I have an idea: Why don't you kids run along? Roman, you take India Rose around the grounds and be sure you show her the waterfall. That'll give you two a chance to catch up with each other.

VESS. And it'll give us a chance to talk about y'all.

ROMAN. Well, would you like to take the grand tour?

INDIA ROSE. If that's all right. Sounds nice.

(They plod off together. **SEYMOUR** *proceeds to follow them off, muttering as he goes…)*

ROMAN. We'll start here. This is the garden. These are plants, and, uh, those are flowers, I guess…

INDIA ROSE. It's foxglove.

ROMAN. Yeah, foxglove.

SEYMOUR. If you want to plant a garden, have it be a vegetable garden – much more manageable, more practical. I wouldn't be caught dead tending the tropic flora.

*(***INDIA ROSE***,* **ROMAN***, and* **SEYMOUR** *exit deeper into the garden.)*

VESS. Oh, I really do hate that we don't get together more often, but I am looking forward to seeing folks. It's been ages! And so many are gone now...

CAMPBELL. Sid Charles.

OPAL. Gone.

VESS. Gerty Allen.

OPAL. Gone.

CAMPBELL. Perry and Angela Hampton.

OPAL. Gone.

VESS. Sherman Carter.

OPAL. Gone.

CAMPBELL. All gone now.

VESS. Even your Edgar. It seems like only yesterday when we would all have the grandest of times together. His loss was so very tragic...

OPAL. Well, everyone was so supportive.

VESS. Oh, Opal, honey. I just hate it all for you, the whole ordeal. You didn't deserve that misfortune...

CAMPBELL. *(catching the Ming vase before it falls)* So, who all did say they were coming?

VESS. It seems so strange, but I reckon we really are taking over now completely from the old guard. The Coterie just won't be the same without all of them. Opal, when are the others getting here?

OPAL. *(falling sands)* I told you, I just don't know. Everybody is so very busy, and I don't expect them all to be able to just drop everything with their families – to come like they used to.

CAMPBELL. I'm sure we'll have a crowd for the Colonel, though. We all love and respect him so well.

OPAL. Maybe...yes, yes. I'm sure they'll be along shortly.

VESS. I couldn't imagine it any other way.

OPAL. You're right. Sometimes I think I make up all these horror stories to tell myself, and there isn't an ounce of truth in any of it.

VESS. There is nothing to be concerned about. You've just worried yourself sick over your daddy, that's all. We got our letter and made plans to come as soon as we could get away; I'm sure plenty of them did, too.

OPAL. You're right, Vess. Really, I wasn't sure about all the addresses. You know, so many folk have moved now, but I sent them anyhow. I even halfway thought about trying to find some of them on the computer, but that just seemed wrong somehow. *(pause)* I was sitting with Daddy earlier, and he didn't really feel like talking so I just sort of sat there with him. I got to thinking about when we were little and Eliza St. Claire died, do you remember?

VESS. We couldn't have been more than eight or ten. I thought I was just gonna die when Mama took me up to visit with her. Swore up and down that woman was King Tut or something close.

OPAL. I remember thinking it was funny: we were all there to watch an old woman die, but it was all just a big party at their house. God! Everyone was so alive.

VESS. And somewhere in all that they picked the Colonel as the patriarch of the Coterie…

OPAL. For weeks I've had dreams about Eliza St. Claire.

CAMPBELL. Well, our wedding was like that. Big old party and each one elbowing around for a place at this table or that. I was just in awe. I didn't know there were so many sun hats in the world.

OPAL. It was a gorgeous wedding…

CAMPBELL. Oh, sure. Even the cake was in tiers, but I didn't have a clue what I'd gotten myself into – hadn' heard the word "Coterie" in my life. I couldn't believe how many "aunts" and "uncles" you had. Course it wasn't until later I found out almost none were related to you or just how appalled they all were that their darling Vess had married an outsider.

VESS. But we haven't really had a get-together like that since then. What happened?

OPAL. Nothing happened. Things just change; people get busy. There'll be other parties. There's always another party.

VESS. You're right, and once we have a new…a little more structure I'm sure we can look on to the future.

*(**INDIA ROSE, ROMAN,** and **SEYMOUR** step back into the garden.* **INDIA ROSE** *hums:* "Sixteen Going on Seventeen.")*

ROMAN. …it used to be there was a gazebo there, but when a tree fell in on it April before last, we just tore the whole thing down. Nobody ever really used it anyway; we just didn't really see the point in rebuilding it.

INDIA ROSE. Oh?

OPAL. There y'all are! Roma, did you show Miss India Rose everything?

ROMAN. I did.

OPAL. Already? Including the waterfall?

ROMAN. I said I did.

OPAL. All right, all right. Well, um, we were just heading in so y'all can just take our place here.

INDIA ROSE. Oh, we don't have to –

VESS. No, no. It's fine. Y'all stay here, and we'll go on in. I'm anxious to see the Colonel anyhow.

(The three adults move to exit. Just before she shuts the door…)

OPAL. *(over the shoulder)* And I'll be back with some tea for y'all shortly. I know you're hot…from your walk.

SEYMOUR. The banquet table is set, but I…I would rather feast on buttermilk and tomato sandwiches.

*(**INDIA ROSE** and **ROMAN** are alone: knowing they are in the right place, they find it hard to situate.)*

INDIA ROSE. It's a shame y'all don't have that gazebo anymore.

ROMAN. Why's that?

INDIA ROSE. I don't know. I love gazebos – always have. They make me think of…

ROMAN. Of what?

INDIA ROSE. No, it's nothing. It's stupid.

ROMAN. What? You can tell me.

INDIA ROSE. I just…fine. I love gazebos because they always remind me of *The Sound of Music*. *(She steps up onto the garden bench.)* Before you say a word, let me say this: I know it's super cliché, but I love it – *(walking down the bench…)* especially when they dance around the gazebo singing with –

(She stumbles and falls; ROMAN *rushes to her.)*

ROMAN. Oh, my God! Are you all right?! Are you hurt? Did you twist your ankle?

INDIA ROSE. No, no. It's fine. I shouldn't have been up there. Really, I'm fine.

(He suppresses a chuckle.)

INDIA ROSE. What are you laughing at? I could be really hurt…

ROMAN. Are you?

INDIA ROSE. No, but I could be.

(She joins his laughter with her own, and they compose a brief symphony of innocent mirth. Quite suddenly, they are much closer to one another's faces than they had been previously.)

ROMAN. What?

INDIA ROSE. Do you remember me?

ROMAN. *(an admission ticket)* A little. You've changed a lot, you know.

INDIA ROSE. It'd be bad if I hadn't. Tell me what you remember.

ROMAN. I – You know how sometimes you're sure you remember things, but it's nothing specific? It's just sort of feelings.

INDIA ROSE. Good stuff, I hope.

ROMAN. Yeah. Good stuff.

INDIA ROSE. Do you know what I remember? Us playing on that old gazebo. I would climb up as high as I could in the rafters and be a princess. Then I'd make you come be a prince and rescue me.

ROMAN. You made me play along?

INDIA ROSE. Well, I couldn't just stay up in the highest room of the tallest tower all my life, could I?

ROMAN. So did I ever come to your rescue?

INDIA ROSE. Every time.

(closer still)

ROMAN. And did I ever kiss you to break the spell?

INDIA ROSE. I can't quite remember…

(**ROMAN** *leans in to break the spell. Only a moment from her lips, he turns away, apparently upset with himself.*)

ROMAN. What're we doing? I'm sorry, but I can't do this.

INDIA ROSE. What?

ROMAN. It's not you – I swear it isn't – I just can't. I don't even know what it is I'm doing or supposed to do or – I don't know. All this.

INDIA ROSE. I'm…I'm…

ROMAN. Please don't be mad. I just don't really know if this is what I want. Or if it's just because it's what they want.

INDIA ROSE. I'm not mad. But Roman, there's nothing wrong with wanting the same thing, is there? They just want us to be happy and safe.

ROMAN. *(beat)* What did you mean: safe?

INDIA ROSE. Just that, you know. Other people aren't quite like us…Haven't you ever watched your friends – just normal people – go out with folks and fall in love and then later get their hearts broken?

ROMAN. *(He has not.)* Yeah…?

INDIA ROSE. Well, whenever that happens to somebody I know, I sort of smile to myself 'cause I know I'm not ever gonna have to go through that. I'll just know, because everybody just knows in the Coterie. Have you ever heard of any of those folks getting divorced?

ROMAN. A lot of them should; staying together doesn't mean they're happy.

INDIA ROSE. No, nobody gets guaranteed to be happy. But when half of marriages end in divorce for everybody else, it is a guarantee to be safe.

ROMAN. Princesses don't get to stay in towers forever.

INDIA ROSE. Once they do get down, they usually marry princes for a reason.

ROMAN. *(slowly, slowly)* I know you're right. Just looking at you, I know you are, but I just –

INDIA ROSE. So take some time to think about it. I'm not in any hurry. It's a lot to go over, but just find me when you have.

ROMAN. *(surprised)* Yeah. Yeah, okay. I think I can handle that.

INDIA ROSE. You're kinda funny, aren't you?

ROMAN. Just a little, but it's sort of like being the tallest leprechaun.

*(Tart and proud, **TESS UNDERWOOD** enters the garden. It would be easy to overlook **JOLENE**'s entrance with her mother.)*

TESS. Yoohoo!!!

ROMAN. *(standing)* Oh, hello…?

TESS. Oh, now don't you even tell me you don't remember me! It might break my heart! Oh, I can't even bear to think you might not remember me! I guess you haven't seen me in a coon's age, though, so I'll allow it this once. I'm your Auntie Tess, silly.

ROMAN. Well, I'm pleased to meet you…again.

TESS. You were so, so little last time I saw you, Ronald.

ROMAN. It's Roman.

TESS. Who is?

ROMAN. Oh, that's my name: Roman.

TESS. The last time I saw you, you were hardly out of diapers!

ROMAN. That so?

TESS. It is; it is. Now, Roman, I know this must be awful hard on you with your grandfather in such a state, but please know that anytime, absolutely anytime you need me or Jo, you're welcome to call on – Oh, my! How silly of me, I've forgotten introductions! Isn't that silly of me?!

ROMAN. Insane.

TESS. You two girls just standing here not knowing what to do. You probably think I'm the rudest person you ever laid eyes on. Well, we can fix that right now.

INDIA ROSE. Oh, I'm –

TESS. My name is Mrs. Tess Underwood – of the Nashville Underwoods – and may I introduce my daughter Miss Jolene Underwood. She's a debutant this season.

(**JOLENE** *steps forward.*)

ROMAN. Lovely to meet you, Miss Jolene.

TESS. *(to* **INDIA ROSE***)* And what are you?

INDIA ROSE. Oh, excuse me. I'm Miss India Rose Johnston. Of the Asheville Johnstons, I suppose.

TESS. *(clabbering)* Oh, it's you. Your parents are here I assume.

INDIA ROSE. Yes, ma'am.

TESS. I see. *(turning to her daughter, touching her hair imperatively and a little too severely)* Jolene dear, I'm sure that you and Roman would like to get caught up. You two were the best of friends as children, after all. *(blank stares)* Jolene, did you even speak?

JOLENE. *(too loudly)* Hi.

ROMAN. It's great to see you again.

JOLENE. It's great.

ROMAN. *(confused)* Would you like to come inside?

JOLENE. Would like.

ROMAN. Are you all right?

JOLENE. I'm…not…

(Her terror is too much, and she hurries off.)

INDIA ROSE. I hope she's okay.

TESS. I'm sure you do…

INDIA ROSE. Ma'am?

TESS. She'll be fine. She probably just went to check on our bags. Awful sweet girl. You'll see what I mean once the two of you get a chance to get reacquainted. She's fine.

INDIA ROSE. Would you like me to go see about her?

TESS. No! *(catching herself)* I'll do that, dear. You can go tell Roman's mother that we're here. Thank you.

ROMAN. *(already making to get away from* **TESS***)* That's alright, Aunt Tess. I can go, too. Why don't you stay here and…have a cup of coffee?

TESS. Well, just as long as you're back here when I get back with Jolene. Roman, I know how keen she was on talking with you…

ROMAN. Yes, ma'am.

*(***ROMAN*** and* **INDIA ROSE** *are gone. Alone,* **TESS** *sits fixing herself a cup of coffee – adding lump after lump after lump of sugar…)*

TESS. Good. Fine. That's fine. Good. Perfect. *(surveying)* Love, love what y'all've done with the place. Letting it…grow out like you have. Sort of a wild look to it…

(After too many lumps of sugar, **VESS** *enters with sweet tea to refresh* **INDIA ROSE** *and* **ROMAN***.)*

VESS. Oh, I hope I'm not interrupting anything! I just thought I might bring y'all a glass of tea to knock the heat off –

(They spot each other. White hat, black hat.)

TESS. *(nose up)* Oh.

VESS. I didn't know you were here yet.

TESS. Hello, Vess.

VESS. Hello, Tess.

TESS. How's Asheville?

VESS. Fine. Nashville?

TESS. Fine.

VESS. Good.

TESS. Good.

(Long, spindly silence. Eyes.)

VESS. Where's your girl?

TESS. With Roman. Yours?

VESS. You're lying through your crooked teeth.

TESS. Think so?

VESS. I know so.

TESS. Well, I think you're wrong.

VESS. Do you?

TESS. I do. So very wrong.

VESS. I'm sorry you feel that way.

TESS. So very sorry.

VESS & TESS. Hmmm…

VESS. I don't have time for this. I'm busy.

TESS. Well…so am I!

VESS. Goodbye, Tess.

TESS. Goodbye.

> *(**VESS** sets down her drink, and both exit. The prehistoric garden is given some Peace at last: a bullfrog croaks, a cicada shudders, and thin yellow light plays on the nimblest fronds. A phone rings several times inside before it is picked up and muffled. **ROMAN** and **JOLENE** find themselves back together, surprised. She is clad bulkily in an outlandish antebellum hoop dress. Seymour – also reappeared – reviews her and speaks.)*

SEYMOUR. I hate to think the way they act in the movies isn't real…real. All that swollen music, those bright smiles, the happy endings. Real.

JOLENE. Umm…hey.

ROMAN. Ahh! Oh, um. Hey.

JOLENE. Heeeey.

ROMAN. You all right?

JOLENE. Oh, I'm fine. You?

ROMAN. I'm good, I guess. You sure you're all right? Your eyes are all puffy...Have you been crying?

JOLENE. No, I – I have pinkeye. *(beat)* So...do you like my dress?

ROMAN. It's very nice.

JOLENE. You think it's stupid, don't you? I told Mama you would, but she said, "No, he'll think you're a true Southern belle." But I asked her, "What if I don't want to be a Southern belle?!" And she told me I didn't have a choice, and I cried, and she told me not to cry and to go put on more make-up.

ROMAN. Jolene!

JOLENE. What?

ROMAN. I like your dress. It's lovely. You're lovely.

JOLENE. You don't have to say that. I know I look stupid.

ROMAN. I know I don't have to, but I do like it. Really.

(They share a moment like a candy bar that so conveniently breaks in two. **JOLENE** *takes both halves.)*

JOLENE. Do you remember me?

ROMAN. A little, but you've changed a lot.

JOLENE. Be bad if I hadn't.

ROMAN. I guess so.

JOLENE. Do you know what I remember best about when we would play together when we were little?

ROMAN. What's that?

JOLENE. The arbor that used to be off to the side over there. I bet you didn't think I'd remember that, did you? No, I have the best memory for things like that. It was a big old arbor, so big we could climb all over it. I'd get in the top and pretend to be a princess under a spell...What happened to it? The arbor?

ROMAN. There wasn't one.

JOLENE. Oh.

ROMAN. There was a gazebo, but it got knocked down last April. A tree fell in on it.

JOLENE. And y'all didn't build it back?

ROMAN. Nobody ever used it.

JOLENE. I bet it was still pretty to look at, though, and I'm sure you had lots of good memories of playing on it.

(She scoots near to him.)

ROMAN. Either way, it's just not there anymore.

JOLENE. Shame. It would give us a little…shade on a hot day like today. And privacy.

ROMAN. What are you –

(In her own way, she tries to kiss him.)

ROMAN. Wh –

(JOLENE kisses him again; she tries, anyway.)

ROMAN. Whoa! You, you can't do that!

JOLENE. *(hysterical)* I…But…I thought you said you like my dress.

ROMAN. I do. Not like that, though. Not that you're not… It's just – I can't do that with you because…because…

JOLENE. Why? What's wrong?

ROMAN. This. All this. I – I can't. I can't do this. Look at you. You're a great girl and all but –

JOLENE. But what? I'm not good enough? Or I'm just not India Rose?

ROMAN. No, listen to me –

JOLENE. I get it. You made up your mind already. I missed my chance, and now I look like a fool.

(Her too heavy make-up begins to wipe itself off.)

ROMAN. No. It isn't you; it isn't anything you've done. It's this. It's like they're trying to breed dogs or horses or something.

(He wrings his hands. JOLENE returns to him, takes his hand.)

JOLENE. Oh, Roman. I know. I know. It seems dumb, and it seems like there's no reason to keep up the Coterie at all, like it's just a bunch of old folks that like to tell stories about their parents.

ROMAN. That's it! You get it. Finally, somebody else gets it; I knew I wasn't crazy. This is all ridiculous, right?

JOLENE. It is, but there's something more, too. Roman, there's always gonna be a Coterie somehow or other. That's sort of what I realized a while back: there'll always be folks that everybody else wants to be. You may as well use being born of them to your advantage if you can.

ROMAN. But – That's just it! By saying that, you're playing right into their game! Look, when I touch your hand I feel you. Warm, soft, human you. A person. Another person in another body.

JOLENE. Just like you.

ROMAN. I think I was expecting you to be made of porcelain or something.

JOLENE. Well, I'm not. I'm just flesh and blood like you.

ROMAN. So don't you see that by forcing us to go through the courting rituals, they're taking that away from us – the human part?

JOLENE. It's a lot easier to just go along with it, you know, Roman.

ROMAN. I know.

(Still visibly fixed on his hands and newly awakened tactile senses...ROMAN eases his hands away from JOLENE.)

ROMAN. I think...I think I need to go take a walk. If you don't mind.

JOLENE. No, sure. That's fine. Fine. Go ahead; I'm just gonna stay here, I guess.

(He is gone.)

Great pick, Mama.

(She has not noticed the appearance of INDIA ROSE in the space.)

INDIA ROSE. Hi, Jolene.

JOLENE. Hello, India.

(Apathetic to the tension, **VESS** *enters presently. She is followed by* **CAMPBELL, OPAL,** *and* **TESS** *in procession.)*

TESS. Oh, there you are, Jo! I've been all over the house looking for you. Sweetheart, where's Roman?

JOLENE. He just did leave –

VESS. *(lips pursed lightly)* Yes, India, what happened to Roman? I thought he was with you.

TESS. Oh, Vess, you poor thing. You must have misheard. He was with Jolene until a few minutes ago. Isn't that right Jolene? They used to play together as children, you know.

VESS. That so? *(a glint of wicked satin stains her eyes)* India, Darleen, why don't you girls run along now and find Roman. I'm sure he just went off to find his mother so y'all could share the big news. Hurry now.

(When they have gone…)

OPAL. Okay, now what's all this about, Vess?

VESS. Well, I hate to steal the children's thunder, but Roman came to Campbell earlier and asked permission to ask our India for her hand.

OPAL. Oh, Vess! Really? I can't even stand it, I'm so excited!

TESS. And what about Jolene?

OPAL. Bless her heart. Tess, you shouldn't worry at all. She has so much going for her. She'll be fine; I just know it.

TESS. Don't you dare give me that. I love you to death, Opal, but don't you dare talk to me like I'm a child.

OPAL. This isn't the end of the world, and there's no need to get bothered.

VESS. You're right: it's never healthy to stew on your misfortunes. Tess, couldn't we bring an end to this bad blood? In light of circumstances.

TESS. Well, that's funny because it doesn't seem like we've settled a damn thing. Actually, all it seems to me is that you've gotten just what you've wanted, and I got stuck with the leftovers. Again. And the worst part, the worst part, Vess, is that you've never seen anything wrong with that.

CAMPBELL. Tess, please.

TESS. Nope. I don't want to hear that from you either, Mr. Johnston. Don't be too shocked now that somebody doesn't want your words of wisdom, but I don't. I'm sure the both of you love to have a laugh with your Asheville socialite friends over your poor widowed sister who can't catch a break in the world. I know you do, but I don't care. Have your laugh! And I'll keep on getting by just like I always have. With or without the white wedding I came here after.

VESS. You can't help love, Tess.

TESS. Ha! Love, ha! That's funny; you're funny. You know you almost sound sincere. Not a one person in the Coterie has married for love in two hundred years. Marriage is about advantage, money, blood; they get love when they take mistresses. I married Ward 'cause he was from the right family and I was happy doing the right thing for myself and for my family. I wanted that for my daughter, too, but you got it for yours instead. So what else is new? *(a beat)* And you keep on standing there like I'm saying something you didn't know. You with your tainted husband. Am I the only one who still remembers his mother?

VESS. Don't you dare say it!

OPAL. Tess, this is neither the time nor the place –

TESS. Has everyone forgotten that his mother was…a Yankee?!

OPAL. Tess! Please, calm down. There is no need.

TESS. Well, I know, I know Eliza St. Claire and the old Coterie would never have stood for it. They would never have trusted you to be matriarch!

VESS. You're being unfair. I never even breathed a word that that's what I was here after.

TESS. Oh, please. You're not fooling anyone. All you'd need is Opal's cooperation, and who wouldn't side with their own in-laws?

OPAL. Now, Tessie –

TESS. Wonderful! This is just wonderful: we left the whole decision to a teenage boy! The fate of the Coterie subject to his whims – Oh, and how silly of me. I didn't realize the whole thing was a set-up from the second we walked in the gate!

VESS. And what about you? Parading your bumpkin daughter in here in that ridiculous dress! She looks like she confused *Gone with the Wind* and *Deliverance*. Don't you tell me you're not after being matriarch just as much as I am!

CAMPBELL. Vess, dear, please.

VESS. Maybe if you weren't so obsessed with keeping score on every little thing, you wouldn't think you had to be such a martyr all the time. Tess, you're never gonna stop feeling like a victim until you stop acting like one.

TESS. What happened to you, Vess? I don't even know who I'm talking to anymore.

VESS. Well, I know exactly what happened to you: you turned into Mama, and you can't stand it. You can't stand the sight of what you did to drive Ward away or what you're doing daily to warp that poor child of yours. I guess that's why you want to be matriarch, too – to validate your own twisted life.

OPAL. Vess, please. I don't mean to get in the middle of all this –

VESS. Clearly.

OPAL. But you have got to stop treating your sister like that. She has handled a hell of a lot more tragedy in her life than you have so cut her a little slack.

VESS. You think I don't know what you're after, too, Opal. You're after being matriarch just as much as we are.

Only difference is you don't need our approval – just our bickering.

OPAL. What do you mean?

VESS. You think if you can keep us from picking a new matriarch before the Colonel dies, you'll just get to ease on in and take over.

OPAL. You think I'm sitting here counting the minutes until my father dies? Is that what you think? Throwing fuel on y'all's quarrel?!

VESS. Vaguely.

OPAL. *(caramel in her teeth)* You're sick. Sure, he may be the Colonel, but don't you forget that he is still my daddy. And, by the way, I know for a fact that he'd be ashamed by the way you've been carrying on since you got here.

CAMPBELL. You can't talk to her like that!

OPAL. My father is dying up in that room, and all you can even think about is who the next matriarch will be. Well, I hate to break it to you, Vess, but look around. Do you see anyone, anyone at all except the four of us? No. They're not here, and they're not coming. They're all gone – extinct – and they didn't leave much for us to fight over.

VESS. What do you mean?

OPAL. Lord, Vess, the phone's been ringing all day: folks calling to say they can't make it. A dozen letters telling me not to look for so-and-so, the Steinems or the Hamptons. Some weren't even opened, just had "return to sender" scrawled across the front.

TESS. And I spoke with Merriam Carter and Cleve Allen, even Gail Bradshaw: they're not coming either.

OPAL. I just thought that more people would…care. Like they used to.

VESS. They do! I know they do. Folk are busy is all. It might have been too short of notice, you sending out the letters.

(A beat. SEYMOUR cannot hold his silence.)

SEYMOUR. I have seen kudzu grow as much as four feet in a day in the middle of summer, but I never knew it to say a word…A child grows up fast and learns to speak even faster. It's hot today – hotter even than I remembered.

TESS. Vess, no. Listen to yourself for a minute. We're all that's left now, and we've got to deal with it ourselves.

OPAL. Which might mean holding off on anybody getting married for a while.

VESS. What's that supposed to mean?

OPAL. I only mean that –

VESS. Oh, I see what's going on here. This is the part where everyone gangs up on Vess. Well, I don't have to stand here and take y'all's hypocrisy or abuse. *(to* **TESS***)* And you! I'll die a happy woman so long as I never set eyes on you again in my life.

TESS. Sounds just fine and dandy to me! *(turns to* **OPAL***)* You've baked some bitter cookies, Opal. Some real bitter cookies.

*(***TESS** *exits.)*

VESS. I'm leaving, and I don't want anyone to come after me.

*(***VESS** *exits deeper into the garden.)*

CAMPBELL. I guess I'd better go after her.

OPAL. I should probably see about Tess in a minute, too.

CAMPBELL. Do you think they'll ever stop?

OPAL. Stop what?

CAMPBELL. Being at each other's throats all the time. I thought sisters were supposed to grow out of that.

OPAL. Who said that?

CAMPBELL. Well, they're actin' like children, aren't they?

OPAL. Who said children grow up? Sometimes it seems like they only just get bigger.

CAMPBELL. I almost don't want to say this, but I guess I'm already saying it. I don't know if you know this or not, but she's been waiting for this for years. She wants so badly to be matriarch. It's what she's wanted more than anything in the world as long as I've known her, and I want it for her.

OPAL. *(waltzing)* We'll just have to wait and see what happens. She deserves it though; she's a good person.

CAMPBELL. No, she's not. I mean, she's not a bad person. She's just not a good one either. She works hard and goes to church and does what's best for our family, but by no means is she a good person.

OPAL. There isn't much more you can ask for.

CAMPBELL. Sure there is! You can be nice or generous or inspiring, or I don't know what…Not that I'm any of those things. I don't really know anybody that is. I know people in movies and books that are, but I don't actually know any myself.

OPAL. Campbell, listen to me – things have a way of working out. If Vess really is the best person to lead the Coterie, then she will.

CAMPBELL. Can I tell you something?

OPAL. Sure. Anything.

CAMPBELL. Please, please don't breathe a word of it to Vess.

OPAL. I won't.

CAMPBELL. Sometimes I wish she wouldn't become matriarch, that Tess or somebody else would, and we would have to go back to Asheville empty-handed. Then if it was Tess, she wouldn't want to have anything to do with the Coterie. We would be out – free – through with all of the politics and gossip. We could just be normal people instead of having to pretend all the time that we're important.

OPAL. Just like our parents told us.

CAMPBELL. Told you. I'm an outsider, remember? Yankee blood.

OPAL. Vess doesn't seem to mind too much.

CAMPBELL. Maybe she is a good person.

OPAL. I've always thought so.

CAMPBELL. *(after a moment)* Well, I guess I ought to go make sure she doesn't break something.

OPAL. I'll go make sure Tess is okay.

(Both begin to exit after the sisters beyond the garden.)

OPAL. Campbell!

CAMPBELL. Hmm?

OPAL. Your secret is safe with me.

CAMPBELL. Thanks.

*(Both take exits. **SEYMOUR** observes the world before announcing:)*

SEYMOUR. I have always been told that it is better to hang pie pans from the eaves to ward off scavengers than to worry over hungry buzzards. Now I am not so sure.

*(**INDIA ROSE** and **ROMAN** enter together, interrupting **SEYMOUR**.)*

ROMAN. ...But that doesn't mean that we have to go on pretending, does it? I mean, how can you when –

*(**JOLENE** enters swiftly, spots **ROMAN**, and proceeds to assault him with a round of light blows.)*

JOLENE. How dare you play with me like that?!

ROMAN. What're you doing?! What's going on? Jolene! What's –

INDIA ROSE. Jolene, stop!

JOLENE. *(still assailing **ROMAN**)* My mama told me you asked India's daddy to marry her! All that rot about porcelain and pretty dresses! Is this porcelain enough for you?!

*(**JOLENE** slaps **ROMAN**. Hard.)*

INDIA ROSE. See, now I'm very confused.

JOLENE. He kissed me after he had already asked to marry you.

ROMAN. No, I – What?! I never asked anybody to marry me!

JOLENE. Are you saying my mama lied?

ROMAN. I'm saying your mama is crazy.

JOLENE. Oh, and yours isn't?

ROMAN. They all are. They think all these people are coming here, but it's still just the four of them.

JOLENE. They really are sort of sad, aren't they? When you think about it.

ROMAN. Yeah.

INDIA ROSE. But they're still our parents. They still just want what's best for us.

JOLENE. That doesn't mean they know.

INDIA ROSE. At least they're trying! All they're doing is what their parents did for them.

ROMAN. Yeah, make them into snobs. They all fight and bicker, but I think deep down they really like it. They like the scandal and arranged marriages. It makes them feel important.

INDIA ROSE. *(less)* It's not all so bad.

ROMAN. It's all fine for you; all you want is a husband that'll come home to you. Somebody you can cook cornbread for.

INDIA ROSE. That's not what it's about! You don't know what you're talking about. That's not what I'm about. *(a beat)* But that doesn't make it wrong.

JOLENE. It does if you do it 'cause you're scared.

INDIA ROSE. *(church mouse)* I don't want that to happen to me.

(**ROMAN** *goes to her, touches her lightly.*)

ROMAN. It won't. Not if we don't let it.

INDIA ROSE. You think they were lying to us the whole time we were growing up?

JOLENE. Sometimes I think there isn't any such thing as growing up; there's only just getting bigger.

INDIA ROSE. Everybody gets bigger sometime.

JOLENE. One day you just get too big to go on any longer – so big you can't hold yourself up any more...just die.

(The tiny bell above tinkles again – lightly. All three gaze up.)

ROMAN. The Colonel is a big man. The biggest.

(Lights lower faintly. SEYMOUR speaks.)

SEYMOUR. Every evening my father would take an after-dinner constitutional around the property or else down the road...to settle himself and to have a moment of Peace, he said. A dozen or so times, he asked me to come along – we never said a word, just walked along, shoulder-to-shoulder. I loved my father: he was a good man.

(A brash cowbell breaks the quiet from offstage. This is not the small, silvery bell heard from the Colonel's room. ROMAN enters, clanging; INDIA ROSE and JOLENE follow him.)

INDIA ROSE. *(hardly audible over the racket)* D'you think they hear us?

(ROMAN continues to summon the adults; OPAL, VESS, and TESS hurriedly charge the already frayed garden. The alarm has been sounded. JOLENE and INDIA ROSE stand together.)

OPAL. What the – Roman! Roman, boy, what are you doing? Put that bell away!

TESS. What's wrong?! What're you doing?

VESS. *(cane syrup)* Roman, dear, please...If you'll put that down a minute and tell us what's the matter. I have a headache coming on...

OPAL. Son, please. He's finally getting some rest up there! You're gonna wake him up! He'll never get back to sleep.

VESS. What has gotten into you, India? Stop that racket!

TESS. Jolene, I told you not to be familiar with that girl...

(Clang, clang.)

VESS. How dare you?!

OPAL. Tess, you have got to take a different tone if you expect –

TESS. Why do I have to tone down if she's doing the same?! I will not tone down –

VESS. Here we go again! It's always my fault!	**OPAL.** Both of you, please! It's not doing any good for you to argue. AND WILL YOU STOP RINGING THAT DAMN COWBELL!!!

(A wall is erected – a wall made from silent bricks and deaf mortar.)

ROMAN. We just wanted to get your attention.

OPAL. Well you've got it. Now it had better be something important.

(Eyes. **SEYMOUR**'s *watch intently.)*

ROMAN. Mom, Aunt Tess, Aunt Vess, we want to talk to y'all. And we don't want you to take it the wrong way, but...

SEYMOUR. *(to audience)* There! There, did you see?

OPAL. But, what, honey?

SEYMOUR. Did you hear what I said? "But." That was it; that was the moment I knew my mother for the first time. *(almost amused)* It's funny, really. It's a tiny word – just three letters – and it can change a life: "I love you, but..." I had wondered where it went.

ROMAN. Well, it's just...all this about marriage and feuds and matriarchs and everything. It's made us realize – *(He looks to* **INDIA ROSE** *and* **JOLENE** *for support, but he is too far gone.)* – that it's not what we want.

OPAL. What, what do you mean? Roman, what does that mean?

ROMAN. It's fine for y'all to have your Coterie parties and to gossip and all, but we don't want to.

OPAL. Sweet'art, I never meant to push you. I love you, and I'm going to be happy as long as you are. However you are.

ROMAN. I just don't think I can go on like you've had to.

OPAL. *(fiddling with her pearls)* It's not so bad. I had you to do it all for. You'll find that out: when you've got a child to hang on for, you can hang on forever.

VESS. I can't believe you, Roman. Do you even realize what your mother has been through to raise you up by herself? And now you start tormenting her when she's already so emotional about your own granddaddy?

TESS. Opal, honey, don't you listen to a word he's said. You have been a sait to bring up that boy and look after the Colonel the way you have. A saint.

OPAL. I just wanted to do right by you, sweetie.

ROMAN. And you have –

OPAL. You just don't want any of what I've tried to give you. Thanks but no thanks.

ROMAN. That's not what I –

OPAL. No, no. You're right. You're an adult. You can make your own choices. I'll support you whatever decisions you make.

(pause)

TESS. I declare! I just don't know what I'd do if my child took that tone with me!

*(**TESS** looks to **JOLENE**; **JOLENE** turns away.)*

JOLENE. I don't want to end up like you and Daddy.

TESS. Your father and I loved each other very much! When we lost him…

JOLENE. Lost him?! Lost him, Mama? Daddy left us!

TESS. How dare you talk to me like that?! Don't you go against your raisin', girl!

*(She looks to **JOLENE**; **JOLENE** turns away.)*

JOLENE. I'm sorry, Mama.

ROMAN. No, you don't have to be sorry anymore. These are our own lives, and I'm not going to apologize for living mine.

INDIA ROSE. And neither am I. You have lied to all of us.

VESS. Oh, Lord have mercy, Opal! You've let that boy talk our children into all kind of craziness...

OPAL. Honey, where is all this coming from? We've all got your best interests in mind.

JOLENE. So you lied about India and Roman getting engaged?

VESS. That wasn't a lie! They are...eventually. And anyway, it's what's best for the both of them.

TESS. Oh, Vess, you're even lower than I thought. You couldn't even bear to think that he might pick Jo over your girl.

ROMAN. Nobody is getting married. Why aren't you listening? This is exactly what I'm talking about: the bickering, the...politics. It's not worth it.

OPAL. When you're older, you'll understand better –

ROMAN. I saw the letters.

OPAL. You what?

ROMAN. I saw the letters. I heard you on the phone earlier. I know it's just y'all that're left.

VESS. You wouldn't understand...

INDIA ROSE. Then explain it! Because right now it looks like you have a tea party, not a Coterie.

OPAL. Then we'll have a tea-party Coterie, but we'll still have it. We owe it to them: to the Colonel and Eliza St. Claire and all of them. And you do, too.

TESS. It's not a question.

JOLENE. We're not going to play y'all's games.

TESS. You will if I say you will.

OPAL. Tess, please.

VESS. No, for once she's right. This is about respect.

INDIA ROSE. You keep telling yourself that, Mama, and see if it turns out true.

OPAL. Roman, why don't we just talk about this another time?

ROMAN. We don't want to turn into y'all!

(long pause)

We've seen you ruin everything you were given, and that's not what we want.

VESS. Well, Opal. Say somthing...

ROMAN. Mama, I didn't mean –

OPAL. *(distant)* Shhh! I think I can hear the kudzu growing.

(A worried **CAMPBELL** *enters frantically, hardly keeping his balance.)*

CAMPBELL. He's gone! He's gone! Opal, he's gone!

OPAL. Who's gone? What's going on?

CAMPBELL. The Colonel! He's not in his room. I was sitting up with him. I guess I sort of dozed off, but when I woke up, he was gone!

(All feel the pain in the soulspace just below their rib cages.)

OPAL. Oh, my God!

TESS. Where could he have gone?!

CAMPBELL. He's not anywhere in the house.

VESS. He couldn't have gone anywhere on his own.

TESS. *(to the younger people)* Well, where is he? Roman? You've made your point, now what did you do with him?

CAMPBELL. How can you say that? They're just children...

TESS. No, they're not.

VESS. This isn't funny, Roman. *(horrified)* India?

OPAL. Listen to yourselves!

VESS. He could be anywhere!

CAMPBELL. What have y'all done?

*(*INDIA ROSE, JOLENE, *and* ROMAN *are silent, dusty mirrors.)*

TESS. Where is the Colonel?! Jolene?!

VESS. What have you done?

OPAL. Roman?

(She shakes her son. He does not move. She adapts.)

OPAL. He can't have gotten far. Let's see where he's got to.

*(*TESS, VESS, *and* CAMPBELL *join in searching, making their rounds calling for the Big Man.)*

OPAL. *(overlapping)* Daddy! Daddy! Colonel! Daddy! Are you out here? Daddy!

VESS. *(overlapping)* Colonel! Colonel Hargrove! Colonel!

TESS. *(overlapping)* Colonel? Colonel, sir! Colonel Hargrove! Where are you?!

CAMPBELL. *(overlapping)* Colonel Hargrove! Colonel, sir! Colonel!

(The no-longer-children remain until a worried INDIA ROSE *crosses to exit.* JOLENE *then exits, searching as well, though not for the Colonel. When* ROMAN *is alone,* SEYMOUR *enters and crosses to him. A big hand holds* ROMAN *in masculine affirmation.)*

SEYMOUR. I had wondered where…These trails twist and turn all out into the woods. They'll take you to Sawyer's Mill, into town, and even to the Interstate now. It's not hard to follow them back, though. I had wondered where…

(He leaves ROMAN *in peace.)*

End of play

SHELF LIFE

by Beth Seeley

SHELF LIFE was presented in a staged reading as part of the Thespian Playworks program at the 2012 Thespian Festival on June 30, 2012. Bill Myatt directed and Judy GeBauer was the dramaturg.

JOSEPHINE .... Kaitlin Thaker
MINERVA ....Megan Sirak
CHARLOTTE ....Keely Kritz
PHOEBE.. Becca Hiiva

ABOUT THE PLAYWRIGHT

Beth Seeley lives in Cincinnati, Ohio with her parents, younger sister, and two cats. She wrote this play during her junior year at Anderson High School and is now a freshmen at Kenyon College where she continues to study theatre and writing. She is forever indebted to her high school theatre director, Chad Weddle; all of the people associated with the Playworks competition, especially Bill Myatt, Judy GeBauer, and Julie Coppens; and her mother, who supported her during every step of the creation of her play.

CHARACTERS

JOSEPHINE - A porcelain doll dressed as a ballerina. Delicate and young, she yearns for something more out of life.

MINERVA - An older porcelain doll dressed in a Victorian gown. She is motherly, conservative, and protective.

CHARLOTTE - A porcelain doll, old and worn and dressed as a clown. Her left leg has been cut off at the knee and replaced by a wooden peg, and the right side of her face is cracked. Charlotte is sweet but eccentric, and always carries a parasol which she affectionately calls "Charlie."

PHOEBE - A porcelain doll dressed in an ornate matador costume. Worldly and passionate, she has a lust for life and adventure.

SETTING

A set of shelves in a child's bedroom in a historic house museum. We see two shelves, one above the other, with an empty space indicating more shelves beneath. Both shelves are filled with antique odds and ends, as well as some children's books from the turn of the last century. The shelves are wood, the edges and corners delicately carved. A music box sits on the lower shelf, stage right, and allows access between the two shelves. In scene two, a string is attached to the bottom of the upper shelf and hangs down into the space below. Each of the actors is playing a nine-inch-tall doll, so the set is sized to fit that scale. We have a closeup view of their miniature world.

Scene 1

*(All three dolls stand still on the shelves. **CHARLOTTE** and **MINERVA** stand posed on the top shelf. **JOSEPHINE** stands on the bottom shelf, with the music box. The lights are dim. Footsteps are heard, seeming to grow nearer. Suddenly a click, and the lights turn on. The dolls do not move. Footsteps fade away.)*

CHARLOTTE. Nothing! *(She tosses her parasol.)*

JOSEPHINE. She hasn't brought anything! Again! Minerva, we've been doing this for nearly a week.

MINERVA. Yes, dear, I know. I know it's difficult. *(begins climbing down to join **JOSEPHINE**)* But there's no need to get so worked up about this. The curator will bring her when she brings her.

JOSEPHINE. But we prepare every day! Organizing, dusting off the shelves...

CHARLOTTE. Winding the music box.

JOSEPHINE. Winding the music box! But every morning it's exactly the same.

MINERVA. *(embraces her)* Patience, Josephine. I know you're anxious. I am too. But we want to look our best for the new arrival, and that takes preparation. A new doll is coming soon, from Europe! I heard the curator discussing it. We want to welcome her into the country with a beautiful new home!

JOSEPHINE. Alright. But all this anticipation is bothering me.

MINERVA. I've noticed.

CHARLOTTE. *(panicked, searching)* Where's Charlie?!

MINERVA. *(calmly)* You tossed him aside, Charlotte. I think he's behind the looking glass.

(**CHARLOTTE** *searches for her parasol behind a full-length mirror and finds it.*)

CHARLOTTE. Ah, yes. (*addressing parasol*) Don't you run off like that again. Had me worried sick.

MINERVA. So, for today I thought we would polish the music box.

JOSEPHINE. (*crossing to the box*) Again? We just cleaned it! It looks fine to me.

MINERVA. What? With our little footprints all over it? Completely unacceptable! (*retrieving a rag from behind the music box*) I think Charlotte chipped some of the paint with that peg leg of hers. It's a wonder the curator hasn't noticed. Everything must be in perfect condition. You wouldn't want the music box to be sent away, would you?

JOSEPHINE. Do you think she would notice one little scratch?

MINERVA. (*holds out the rag*) Polish! And get Charlotte to help you. (*starts climbing up the music box to the upper shelf.*) I'm going to see if the curator has moved upstairs.

(**MINERVA** *walks to the far left side of the top shelf. She peers out, watching someone far off in another room.* **JOSEPHINE** *and* **CHARLOTTE** *begin polishing the music box.* **MINERVA** *steps back.*)

MINERVA. She's not in sight. I think a little music might be safe. Josephine, would you start it up for us?

(**JOSEPHINE** *nods and turns the music box key. She releases, and a delicate tune fills the air.*)

MINERVA. Splendid!

(**MINERVA** *stands serenely looking at the box, humming the tune quietly.* **CHARLOTTE** *stops polishing and holds her parasol as if it were her dance partner. She attempts a jerky waltz.*)

CHARLOTTE. Careful, Charlie! Can't dance like I used to. Darn leg moving every which way.

JOSEPHINE. Here, Charlotte, I'll dance with you. I hope you don't mind if I step in, Charlie.

CHARLOTTE. *(setting the parasol against the music box)* He never was much for dancing anyway.

(**CHARLOTTE** *and* **JOSEPHINE** *waltz.* **MINERVA** *walks to the opposite side of the shelf, still humming, staring into the distance.)*

CHARLOTTE. *(breaking from* **JOSEPHINE***)* No more. You go on, I'll polish. *(She picks up her rag.)*

JOSEPHINE. Watch this, Charlotte. I've been practicing. *(She twirls gracefully.)*

CHARLOTTE. The girl's a whirling top!

(**JOSEPHINE** *spins and twirls to the music, moving toward the music box until she smacks into it. The song abruptly stops.)*

MINERVA. Josephine! What have I told you about spinning around so carelessly? You're going to damage yourself!

JOSEPHINE. I was trying to be careful. I just got wrapped up in the music, that's all.

MINERVA. The last time you got "wrapped up in the music" you almost ripped your dress. How many times have I told you that you need to be in pristine condition for the curator to keep you on display?

JOSEPHINE. You always say that, but what about Charlotte?

MINERVA. Charlotte is special.

JOSEPHINE. Well I wouldn't keep hitting things if there were more room to move!

MINERVA. Then don't move so much! Do you think there will be any room to move in storage? Back in the dark, packed in boxes full of sawdust? You can't breathe, you can't see, and you definitely can't dance.

(The sound of a door opening startles them.)

JOSEPHINE. She's coming back.

MINERVA. Quickly girls!

(**MINERVA** *and* **JOSEPHINE** *assume their poses.* **CHARLOTTE** *darts frantically around, searching for Charlie.* **JOSEPHINE** *picks up the parasol and hands it to* **CHARLOTTE**, *who then climbs to the top shelf. All three dolls pose. Footsteps approach.* **PHOEBE** *is placed on the bottom shelf beside* **JOSEPHINE**. *The footsteps begin again and fade. Silence.* **JOSEPHINE** *and* **PHOEBE** *turn to face each other, looking each other over.* **CHARLOTTE** *peers down over the edge to observe the new arrival.* **MINERVA** *quickly climbs to the lower shelf.*)

MINERVA. Welcome, welcome! *(surprised by* **PHOEBE**'*s strange dress)* My name is Minerva. This is Josephine, and this is... *(looking around)* Charlotte! Charlotte, are you coming?

CHARLOTTE. *(nervously calls down)* I can't! I'm not ready!

MINERVA. Yes you are, dear! You're perfectly fine! Come down and bring Charlie!

(**CHARLOTTE** *slowly begins climbing down, clutching her parasol tightly.*)

I wasn't expecting you at this time of day. Newcomers usually arrive either at night or in the early morning. That's when Charlotte and Josephine came, you see. They were both morning deliveries. Oh, but I'm sorry, I haven't even asked your name!

PHOEBE. Phoebe. *(shakes both their hands)* Pleased to meet you both.

JOSEPHINE. What is that costume you're wearing? It's like nothing I've ever seen before. Well, not to say that I've seen much...

PHOEBE. It's classic bullfighting attire, from Spain. *(offering her sleeve to* **JOSEPHINE**) Like the spangles?

JOSEPHINE. *(entranced)* They're beautiful.

MINERVA. Certainly a very...interesting choice of attire for a young lady.

(**CHARLOTTE** *has wandered over and is admiring* **PHOEBE**'*s outfit from afar.*)

PHOEBE. Hello there! You must be Charlotte. My name's Phoebe. I am happy to make your acquaintance.

(**CHARLOTTE** *makes no response.*)

That's a lovely parasol you have there.

JOSEPHINE. She calls it "Charlie."

PHOEBE. I'm very pleased to meet you, Charlie. *(She bows deeply, then stands and looks at* **CHARLOTTE,** *speaking quietly.)* Do I know you from somewhere?

(**CHARLOTTE,** *overcome with emotion, turns and scrambles up the music box.)*

PHOEBE. Oh. I hope I didn't offend her.

MINERVA. Charlotte often behaves strangely. It's one of the things you'll get used to, living here.

PHOEBE. *(to* **JOSEPHINE***)* What happened to her leg?

JOSEPHINE. I don't really know. Her leg broke off and the side of her face cracked somehow before she came here, but she's never spoken about it. When I've asked her where she used to live, she says she can't remember. *(grinning)* I think she must've fallen on her head.

MINERVA. *(reprimanding)* Josephine! Phoebe, why don't you let us tell you about your new home?

PHOEBE. Alright.

MINERVA. The house was built in 1874. Two generations had lived here before it was turned into a museum in 1906. Most things here belonged to the original owners, except for a few special finds. *(smiles at the girls)*

PHOEBE. *(indicating the music box.)* What's this?

MINERVA. That's an old music box that used to belong to the family. Beautiful, isn't it? We can play it all we want when there's no one around.

PHOEBE. The detail work is gorgeous. I've seen a few like this one, but never with so many intricate paintings.

JOSEPHINE. Where were you kept before you came here?

PHOEBE. I've moved around a lot. I'm not even sure how many times. Lots of people like to keep music boxes, I've discovered. I figure at this point I'm a regular connoisseur.

MINERVA. Well, I hope this one suits your refined tastes, as it's the only one we have.

PHOEBE. Oh definitely, it's beautiful. There seem to be a few scuff marks though…

JOSEPHINE. That's because we climb on top of the music box to reach the upper shelf. Do you want to see?

PHOEBE. Sure!

> (JOSEPHINE *climbs to the top, followed by* PHOEBE. MINERVA *frantically scrubs at a spot on the box, and then climbs up after the girls.*)

JOSEPHINE. Up here we have more antiques and a few children's books, as well as a better view of the adjoining room! *(indicates off stage left, toward the audience)* Which is…exciting.

PHOEBE. Where else do you go? *(All look at* PHOEBE *in confusion.)* Where else in the museum? Or at least on the rest of these shelves?

MINERVA. We don't go anywhere else. We stay here.

PHOEBE. All day? What about at night, when the visitors and the curator are gone?

MINERVA. That would be far too dangerous, we could be hurt. You see, we're only allowed to be kept on display because we're in such good condition. All these antiques are flawless. Scratched or damaged items are sent to storage.

PHOEBE. Charlotte looks like she's had a few bruises in her day.

MINERVA. That's none of your business.

PHOEBE. Right, sorry. So what is storage, exactly?

MINERVA. I simply suggest that you remain on these shelves, and don't risk your life for the sake of curiosity. *(Flustered, she turns away to attend to* CHARLOTTE.*)*

JOSEPHINE. *(quietly, to* **PHOEBE***)* Minerva lived with the families in this house before it became a museum. When they moved away, they left her here with most of the other things. While the house was being renovated, she was stuck in storage for months. She didn't know what was going on, and she thought she had been abandoned forever. That is, until she was brought out and put here. Minerva told me there were other dolls in storage, but none of them looked as new as she did. She made it out, but all the rest are still back there, I guess. She says it was horrible, even for a few months. I can't imagine how the others must feel.

PHOEBE. Well you look as clean as a whistle, so there's nothing for you to worry about.

JOSEPHINE. As long as I stay here. Minerva is right, you could easily break yourself climbing on these shelves. The music box is the only reason we're able to go between the two.

PHOEBE. *(peering down, over the edge of the shelf)* It wouldn't be that difficult... When does the museum close?

JOSEPHINE. It should be lights out in about four hours.

PHOEBE. Is that a clock on that wall?

JOSEPHINE. Yes. But the point is that you'll fall and break–

PHOEBE. *(beginning to lower herself down from the shelf)* I'll be back soon, don't worry! Bye, Josephine. *(She lets go, and vanishes.)*

MINERVA. *(turning)* Phoebe? Stop! Phoebe! *(***PHOEBE** *is gone.)* Well I never! Such a foolish–what right does she have to come to our home and immediately disobey our most basic principles? You can't just leave and go wherever you please without any regard for the consequences! She'll end up in storage for sure! I– *(regaining control)* I'm turning in early, ladies. When that girl– *If* Miss Phoebe returns tell her that I will not speak to her until the morning. Good night.

(She walks to her place and poses. **JOSEPHINE** *and* **CHARLOTTE** *stand side by side, looking in the direction that* **PHOEBE** *left.)*

JOSEPHINE. I hope she makes it back. If she does, things are sure to get a lot more interesting around here.

(blackout)

Scene 2

(JOSEPHINE sits alone on the bottom shelf. Both MINERVA *and* CHARLOTTE *are in their poses on the top. She is startled when she notices* PHOEBE *climbing up onto the bottom shelf from below, carrying a sack.)*

JOSEPHINE. Phoebe! What are you doing back so late? You've been gone for three hours!

PHOEBE. With plenty of time before the curator checks in on us. Can you give me a hand?

JOSEPHINE. *(as she is pulling* PHOEBE *up)* You shouldn't have run off like that. Minerva was right, it's extremely dangerous!

PHOEBE. Yes, I gathered that. But I'm back, aren't I? It's fine. This old house is beautiful, I can't believe you've hardly seen any of it. Look, I brought some stuff back. *(begins to unfold her matador cape, tied like a handkerchief)*

JOSEPHINE. Minerva and Charlotte are asleep. Minerva says she won't talk to you until the morning. I don't think I blame her.

PHOEBE. I just did some exploring, that's all. You should try it sometime. There are tons of things to see. Here we go, I got you something. *(pulls a large notepad and pencil from the bag)* A notepad I found and a bit of a pencil. There you go, Josie.

JOSEPHINE. "Josie." What kind of a name is that?

PHOEBE. It's short for Josephine! Do you mind if I call you that?

JOSEPHINE. Not at all! *(covering her outburst)* I mean, if you want. So, what will I put in this?

PHOEBE. Whatever you want! Like drawings, or stories!

JOSEPHINE. Oh, I don't know how to write a story.

PHOEBE. It's easy! Write about the things you do during the day. What do you do during the day?

JOSEPHINE. Uh…plenty! I read books. Well, re-read them because I've gone through all of these ones already. I listen to the music box. I dance when Minerva lets me, or when she's not paying attention. And then, Minerva always has us clean something... That's not very much to write about, is it?

PHOEBE. That's fine, but I'm getting the sense you need to get out more often.

JOSEPHINE. I thought we went over this. There's no way I'm climbing off these shelves! I'm not some experienced acrobat like you. With my luck I'll end up breaking a leg and you'll never see me again! How did you get so good at climbing, anyway?

PHOEBE. Experience. I've scaled toy boxes, climbed up shelves at pawnshops... I have good balance too. I was on a ship once.

JOSEPHINE. How did you get to all those places?

PHOEBE. Here's my secret, Josie. When I get tired of living someplace, I just leave.

JOSEPHINE. *(shocked)* You leave?

PHOEBE. Just walk out.

JOSEPHINE. But don't– But doesn't your family miss you? How do you know where to go? What if you get lost?

PHOEBE. Sometimes I guess they miss me, but usually I leave after they've forgotten about me. When no one's playing with me anymore, I know it's time to go.

JOSEPHINE. People play with you?

PHOEBE. Yeah, little kids would play with me, or maybe some woman would buy different outfits for me. That's where I got this little number. Or sometimes I'd just be put on a shelf to be admired. But I always go exploring, there's no point in standing here all day.

JOSEPHINE. What kind of places have you been to? Can you– Can you tell me what a ship looks like? They've been mentioned in a few of the books, but I'm not sure.

PHOEBE. Certainly! *(indicates that* **JOSEPHINE** *take a seat)* I'll tell you about the first time I ever saw one. Gosh, it was a while ago. Let's see... A girl named... Ellen was carrying me in her bag as she walked with her family along the docks. *(seeing* **JOSEPHINE**'s *confusion)* Docks are places on the ocean where ships are kept when they're not sailing. Oh, do you know what the ocean is?

JOSEPHINE. Yes, I've read about that! Isn't it a big bunch of water?

PHOEBE. Yeah, basically. There's so much of it, stretching on and on for miles! And it moves constantly: rocking gently with little waves, or sloshing and churning when storm winds pick up. The water is usually a deep blue-green in the sunlight, but it changes with the color of the sky...

JOSEPHINE. And the ships?

PHOEBE. Ah, yes. So I looked outside the bag, and saw these huge, wooden structures floating in the water. They're rounded on the bottom, and flat on the top, with high, wooden towers that reach to the sky, and attached to those is massive white cloth that ripples in the wind. I thought to myself, "I need to get onto one of those things!" So I climbed out of Ellen's bag, and scampered up a wooden plank that led from the dock to the top of a ship. I hid behind some some barrels. *(off* **JOSEPHINE**'s *quizzical expression)* Round, wooden... cylinders, just as a man walked by. I was scared, Josie, but I was excited too! The man must've caught sight of something blue behind the barrel–I was wearing a ball gown then–because he picked me up. He had a bushy grey beard, and bright green eyes lined with wrinkles. He looked surprised, but then he smiled at me, said I reminded him of his daughter. He put me on a shelf in his cabin. We sailed for months, until we arrived at our destination. When he met his daughter at the port he gave me to her. Never saw a happier little girl.

JOSEPHINE. Was it nice? Sailing?

PHOEBE. Not at first. The ship rocked all the time and I could hardly stay upright. Sometimes there were terrible storms and I was sure we would sink, but

Captain Gibson got us through all right. That was the man's name. You could look out and see nothing but water for miles. I heard sea birds call every morning, and I could smell the ocean.

JOSEPHINE. What does it smell like?

PHOEBE. Salt, mostly. Kind of unpleasant, but that's not the point. The point is that I'll remember those few months for the rest of my life, and you should have something like that too.

JOSEPHINE. Phoebe, I'm happy here. I have a home with Minerva and Charlotte. People come to look at me all the time, I'm very much appreciated. It's safe.

PHOEBE. Safe? You mean, being trapped up here on a shelf so that you spend your whole life gathering dust instead of doing anything? Is being "safe" that important to you? Or is that what Minerva believes and she's brainwashed you into thinking that way?

JOSEPHINE. I dont understand. Brain–?

PHOEBE. …washed. It means that she's forced you into agreeing with her and doing what she wants even if you know it's wrong.

JOSEPHINE. Minerva hasn't… *(unaccustomed to the term)* washed my brain with anything! I've seen antiques taken off to storage, I know it exists. Not one of them has come back, Phoebe. Why should I listen to you, anyway? You don't have a home! You don't know what it's like to have someone care about you so you think it's wrong! I don't want your ships, or your far-off places, or your fancy clothes. In fact, if you can leave whenever you want then I think you should–

PHOEBE. *(noticing that* **CHARLOTTE** *has climbed down to the lower shelf and is standing near)* Hello, Charlotte.

JOSEPHINE. Ch-Charlotte! I didn't see you there. You can come over here if you'd like. I'm sorry I woke you up.

CHARLOTTE. *(walks over and sits beside the open bag)* You brought something back. What is it?

PHOEBE. *(kneeling beside her)* I brought back a few things, actually. A journal, for Josie, a piece of string to make climbing the bookcase easier, and this for you. *(She pulls out a large loop of beads, big enough to wear as a sash.)* It's a bracelet. I want to apologize for upsetting you earlier.

CHARLOTTE. *(takes the bracelet, doesn't put it on)* I don't like your new clothes. Too flashy.

PHOEBE. My new–?

CHARLOTTE. Charlie. Do you remember Charlie?

PHOEBE. You introduced me to him earlier today–

CHARLOTTE. Don't you remember? ...I'd forgotten.

JOSEPHINE. Charlotte, who are you talking about? Do you need to go back to sleep?

CHARLOTTE. *(to **PHOEBE**)* You knew Charlie. We both did.

PHOEBE. Charlie...was a boy...in his room...with the toy box?!

CHARLOTTE. *(through tears)* Yes, yes!

PHOEBE. Charlotte! *(They embrace.)* What happened to you?

CHARLOTTE. He dropped me. *(She starts to sob.)*

PHOEBE. He– He dropped you?

CHARLOTTE. In a big crowd. And then I couldn't find him. People were screaming and I couldn't hear his voice. Someone stepped on me. I could hear my leg crunch, but I couldn't hear Charlie. *(continues to cry)*

JOSEPHINE. *(attempting to calm **CHARLOTTE**)* Charlotte, Phoebe what's going on?

PHOEBE. I'll explain what I know. For a time, Charlotte and I both owned by the same boy. He had a collection of...

CHARLOTTE. *(whimpers)* Circus figures.

PHOEBE. Right. I was a tightrope walker then. He owned Charlotte long before he got me, but when I arrived we all lived together.

CHARLOTTE. He got me this parasol. My Charlie...

PHOEBE. A few months into my stay, I heard his parents talking about going on some long trip. I wasn't interested in being left in an empty house for weeks on end, so a few days later I headed out. Charlotte was his favorite doll, and he took her along.

JOSEPHINE. Where did Charlie take you, Charlotte?

CHARLOTTE. *(through tears)* A big, big boat. Lots of people. It was nice. Until something happened one night that made everyone upset. They started running around yelling something about ice. I didn't understand, everything happened so fast! There were so many people pushing us around. Charlie dropped me in the crowd. A girl stepped on me, smashed my leg, but she picked me up. We got onto a smaller boat, only big enough to fit a few people. Everyone was crying. The girl held me close. I never saw Charlie again. *(looks up with wide eyes)* He was a good boy. I was happy then. I had forgotten for years. Kept the thoughts away.

PHOEBE. I could tell you were his favorite, Charlotte.

CHARLOTTE. I was, wasn't I? *(puts the beads on)* Thank you, Phoebe. Goodnight. *(climbs back to her place on the top shelf)*

JOSEPHINE. I never knew. She never talked about where she used to live.

PHOEBE. Charlie loved all his toys. He played with us every day. He always had some new adventure planned. I enjoyed living there. It was a good home.

JOSEPHINE. It does sound nice.

(Shuffling is heard in another room.)

Sounds like the curator is locking up. She'll be here soon, let's go to sleep.

(They get into their positions on the shelf.)

PHOEBE. You should come down with me tomorrow.

JOSEPHINE. I don't think so.

(Footsteps come closer, light shuts off. Footsteps fade.)

JOSEPHINE. Goodnight, Phoebe.

PHOEBE. Goodnight, Josie.

Scene 3

(The lights are dim onstage, as if the lamp is out, but there are morning rays shining onto the bookshelf. **MINERVA** *and* **CHARLOTTE** *are stationary on the upper portion of the shelves. The bottom shelf is empty.* **JOSEPHINE** *climbs onto the bottom shelf from below, followed by* **PHOEBE**.*)*

JOSEPHINE. Hurry, Phoebe. Come on!

PHOEBE. I'm right behind you. And watch where you're stepping!

JOSEPHINE. Sorry!

(Pulls **PHOEBE** *up. They lay down on the shelf, out of breath.* **JOSEPHINE** *starts to giggle, and* **PHOEBE** *soon joins in. They both lie there, trying to stifle their laughter.)*

JOSEPHINE. Shhh, we're going to wake up Minerva!

PHOEBE. We've been way louder than this before. I don't think she'll notice.

JOSEPHINE. Those dresses were amazing!

PHOEBE. The ones hanging in the bedroom? Yeah, they were pretty beautiful.

JOSEPHINE. I wish I could fit into one. I'm sick of this ballerina outfit. I've been wearing it for years. The red gown was nice, don't you think?

PHOEBE. Red would look good on you. Oh, I almost forgot! *(holds up a brooch)*

JOSEPHINE. How'd you get that?!

PHOEBE. Found it on a dressing table. I think I'll give it to Charlotte.

JOSEPHINE. No, Minerva will see it! I feel bad that I haven't told her about the last five nights.

PHOEBE. So tell her. She sees me leave the shelves every day.

JOSEPHINE. I know, but it's different. She doesn't expect me to do this kind of thing.

PHOEBE. Josie, if Minerva cares about you, she'll let you do what makes you happy.

JOSEPHINE. Maybe I'll tell her in the morning. *(begins re-lacing her ballet shoes and notices something wrong)* There's a run in my tights! I must have gotten them caught on something!

PHOEBE. Let me see. **(JOSEPHINE** *reveals the back of her leg.)* Oh, you're right. But it doesn't look that bad, it's a small run.

JOSEPHINE. Someone will see! Minerva, or the curator! Phoebe, I'll be sent into storage!

PHOEBE. No one is going to notice, you'll be fine! Josie, you've got to calm down or you'll really wake up Minerva.

MINERVA. Wake me up for what?

(The two girls struggle for words.)

To tell me that you've been leaving with Phoebe? I began to suspect something was wrong about two days ago. You seemed so tired during the day, and I would hear strange noises at night. I should have realized...

PHOEBE. *(approaching* **MINERVA***)* Don't blame Josie, I asked her to come with me. But it's been perfectly safe and–

MINERVA. *(noticing how* **JOSEPHINE** *is hiding her leg)* What's this? Josephine, what are you hiding from me?

JOSEPHINE. Minerva I–

MINERVA. *(grasping her leg, then dropping it in shock)* How could you do this to me? How could you do this to yourself? Ever since you came here I have been working to keep you safe, and this is how you repay me?

JOSEPHINE. *(frightened)* I'm sorry, Minerva.

MINERVA. You've risked losing everything you have here! Risked tearing apart our family!

JOSEPHINE. *(through tears)* I promise I won't leave again!

MINERVA. I never expected this from you, Josephine. Don't you know I'm just trying to protect you?

JOSEPHINE. I know. I'm sorry I disobeyed you. I was wrong.

MINERVA. *(gently, comforting)* My sweet, foolish little girl. I just want you home.

JOSEPHINE. I am home. To stay.

MINERVA. That's my girl. We'll sort this out tomorrow.

(**JOSEPHINE** *nods and gets into her pose.* **MINERVA** *walks towards the music box.*)

MINERVA. Phoebe? May I speak to you up here?

(**PHOEBE** *nods, and follows* **MINERVA** *up the music box onto the top shelf.*)

MINERVA. *(to* **CHARLOTTE***)* Charlotte, dear. May Phoebe and I have a moment alone?

(*She sends* **CHARLOTTE** *down the music box.*)

PHOEBE. Minerva, the run really isn't that bad. There was no need to scare Josie that way–

MINERVA. I want you to leave.

PHOEBE. Minerva, listen–

MINERVA. I would tell you to get out now, but Josephine would see. And I don't want her to make any choices she might regret. You will leave tomorrow night.

PHOEBE. You don't have to get so upset. She is going to be fine!

MINERVA. Oh, really? Will she be fine the next time you run about the house without my permission, or the next? It may be a small run now, but who knows what could happen to her out there. You may not care about your own safety, but at least care about Josephine.

PHOEBE. I do care about Josephine! That's why I'm doing this! She hates being cooped up here, and I want to help her experience the rest of the world.

MINERVA. Help her? Please, don't be so self-righteous. You are dragging her around for your own entertainment, and she's the one who's going to have to suffer for it. I will not have Josephine sent to storage because of your selfishness!

PHOEBE. I'm selfish? You're the one who insists on manipulating her into a submissive, frightened, lifeless...mannequin!

MINERVA. I have given her a family! Something you could never understand!

PHOEBE. Josephine needs to make her own decisions, but you're holding her back because you're too afraid to be alone!

MINERVA. Don't you say another word–

PHOEBE. You're choking the life out of her, so someday she'll be just as bitter as you!

MINERVA. Phoebe, this is my home and I order you to be silent!

PHOEBE. It's not storage that Josephine should be afraid of.

MINERVA. Get out of my sight!

(**PHOEBE** *climbs to the lower shelf as the lights fade to black.*)

Scene 4

(It's daytime. The light is on. **JOSEPHINE** *and* **PHOEBE** *are on the top shelf with large rags, cleaning the wood and dusting the antiques.* **MINERVA** *is polishing the music box while* **CHARLOTTE** *dusts on the lower shelf.* **CHARLOTTE** *is now wearing both the bracelet and brooch.)*

PHOEBE. Hey, Josie?

JOSEPHINE. Yes?

PHOEBE. *(hesitates, then indicates the wood she's been cleaning)* How does this look?

JOSEPHINE. Fine. But you're missing a smudge over there.

(pause as **JOSEPHINE** *returns to her work)*

PHOEBE. I'm going to be leaving soon.

JOSEPHINE. Why?

PHOEBE. I've got to move on. Tonight.

JOSEPHINE. Is this because I won't leave the shelf with you any more?

PHOEBE. No, it's not your fault. It's just–

MINERVA. *(calling from below)* Is everything alright up there?

JOSEPHINE. Yes, we're fine, thank you! *(to* **PHOEBE***)* Minerva's just anxious about me, and I told her I won't leave anymore, that's all she wants.

PHOEBE. If I keep climbing then you will too! I know that, Minerva knows that, and you know that. But I can't stay up here, so–

JOSEPHINE. So you're leaving me alone? Phoebe, you're the best friend I've ever had. Even Charlotte's happier because you're here! How can you leave now?

PHOEBE. I'm trying to help you! To keep you safe! Isn't that what you want?

JOSEPHINE. Am I supposed to choose between staying up here or being with you? Excuse me, Phoebe, but that doesn't seem fair.

(CHARLOTTE has wandered to the far edge of the bookshelf in order to look into the next room)

CHARLOTTE. The curator is coming!

(They scramble to their places; CHARLOTTE removes her accessories. Footsteps grow closer. Light shuts out. Footsteps fade. PHOEBE begins shuffling around, setting up the string for her descent.)

JOSEPHINE. So this is it. Where are you going to go?

PHOEBE. I saw a pawn shop two blocks down the street. I can make it there before dawn.

JOSEPHINE. I still can't believe you're leaving. Things will just go back to the way they were. I'll miss you.

PHOEBE. So come with me.

JOSEPHINE. You mean to the pawn shop?

PHOEBE. Yeah. We can go together.

JOSEPHINE. Away from Charlotte and Minerva…

PHOEBE. Away from this shelf.

JOSEPHINE. Away from my home! But…

PHOEBE. Did you like it down there? In the rest of the museum?

JOSEPHINE. It was amazing. But it was frightening.

PHOEBE. Isn't that what made it amazing? You're a special person, Josephine. I know Minerva says that too, but she thinks that special things should be kept up on shelves. And I think she's wrong. Leave with me.

JOSEPHINE. I don't know, Phoebe. You're asking me to decide so quickly. Can't I have a little more time?

PHOEBE. I have to go tonight, but I'll leave the string so you can follow me if you want. I wish you would.

JOSEPHINE. Phoebe I–

(PHOEBE pulls her into a hug. They embrace for a moment in silence. PHOEBE pulls away and begins to climb down.)

PHOEBE. *(calling up as she descends)* Remember, two blocks over! On the right!

JOSEPHINE. Okay, I'll remember! *(She watches* **PHOEBE** *climb.)* You know, Phoebe, I always admired–

PHOEBE. The string! Josie, it's breaking! I've got to come back up!

JOSEPHINE. All right, come on, hurry!

PHOEBE. It's too far! Josie!

JOSEPHINE. *(reaching her hand down)* Phoebe!

(The string breaks. **PHOEBE** *screams.)*

Phoebe!

(The sound of shattering porcelain is heard far below. Lights shut off.)

Scene 5

(Lights up on JOSEPHINE *seated in the same place she was when* PHOEBE *fell.* MINERVA *shuffles about on the upper shelf.* CHARLOTTE *limps across the lower shelf to* JOSEPHINE. *She is wearing the gifts* PHOEBE *gave her.)*

CHARLOTTE. You've been sitting here a long time.

JOSEPHINE. Yeah, I know.

CHARLOTTE. You miss her?

JOSEPHINE. Charlotte, before Phoebe went down, she asked me to come with her. If I had climbed down that string, I would be dead, too.

CHARLOTTE. Why didn't you go?

JOSEPHINE. I was afraid.

CHARLOTTE. It is dangerous.

JOSEPHINE. We never had a problem before. *(through tears)* She shouldn't have left. She could have stayed here.

CHARLOTTE. This is not the life she wanted.

JOSEPHINE. Well now she doesn't have a life at all! *(sobs)*

CHARLOTTE. *(takes off her bracelet and brooch, draping the bracelet around* JOSEPHINE*'s neck and pinning the brooch to her shirt)* I miss Charlie. Losing him was the worst thing that ever happened to me. I couldn't bear his absence, so I forgot all the times we had been together. Now I see the memories of my life with Charlie are worth everything I've been through. I'm glad Phoebe came here. I'm glad I remember.

(She limps away, twirling her parasol. JOSEPHINE *caresses the bracelet and broach, weeping softly.* MINERVA *has also climbed down the music box, and is now approaching* JOSEPHINE.*)*

MINERVA. Feeling any better this morning?

JOSEPHINE. Not much.

MINERVA. These things take time. You'll feel better eventually.

JOSEPHINE. Why did you tell her to leave?

MINERVA. Did Phoebe tell you that?

JOSEPHINE. I could put two and two together. If Phoebe was going into the rest of the house, you knew I would, too.

MINERVA. And am I right?

JOSEPHINE. Yes. I liked going down there with her. It was exciting.

MINERVA. I'm sure. But now you see what that leads to.

JOSEPHINE. I never thought it would lead to this!

MINERVA. Exactly, Josephine! You didn't think! You ignored everything I've told you about leaving the shelves so you could follow that foolish girl and her romantic fantasies! And now she's dead. Is this what you want for yourself? *(grabs bracelet)* Do these trinkets mean so much to you that you're willing to kill yourself?!

JOSEPHINE. No! That's not what it's about! It's not about the bracelets or the toys–it's about how you feel. The freedom. It's about seeing things that you could never imagine in your tiny little world! It was being with Phoebe, and it was experiencing life! I used to feel sorry for Charlotte because she isn't perfect the way I am. She's broken. But now I don't feel sorry for her. I envy her! Before she came here, she had a life that she enjoyed. She played with a boy who loved her and took her on wonderful adventures! Yes, they lost each other, but while they were together she had a reason to get up every morning. What reason do we have?

MINERVA. We are here for the museum.

JOSEPHINE. What has the museum done for us? We've been kept up on this shelf for years for people to gawk and stare at! No one touches us or plays with us. I stay because I'm afraid. I'm afraid of storage, of being packed away in a box, forgotten and unloved. But I don't think that storage is so different from where we are right now, doing nothing with ourselves! You and I and Charlotte are all going to become brittle and

cracked at some point. One day we are going to die.
And when we do, what will our lives have meant to
us? What will my life mean to me? Phoebe saw ships
floating on deep blue water. She knew children
who laughed and played with her, and she heard
the music from many, many music boxes. She died
because of the way she lived. But I would rather rot
tomorrow at the bottom of the ocean, than live my
whole life having never seen the sea. I have to leave.
(walks to **CHARLOTTE***)* Goodbye Charlotte, Charlie.

CHARLOTTE. This isn't Charlie. But it does remind me of
him. *(The two embrace.)*

MINERVA. Where are you going to go?

JOSEPHINE. Two blocks over, on the right. Goodbye,
Minerva. *(She prepares to climb down.)*

MINERVA. You can't make it down. The string snapped.

JOSEPHINE. Phoebe climbed down once without the string.
I can do it too.

MINERVA. And how will you manage that, Josephine? You'll
kill yourself!

JOSEPHINE. I don't know. Wish me luck!

CHARLOTTE. *(cranking the music box)* Good luck!

(**MINERVA** *glares at her.*)

(The music begins to play. **CHARLOTTE** *crosses to stand
next to* **MINERVA.** **JOSEPHINE** *begins her descent. The
two older dolls watch her leave as the stage fades to
black.)*

End of Play

www.ingramcontent.com/pod-product-compliance
Lightning Source LLC
Chambersburg PA
CBHW070329120726
47909CB00008B/2661